Robert Williams Buchanan, Dalziel Brothers

North Coast And Other Poems

Robert Williams Buchanan, Dalziel Brothers

North Coast And Other Poems

ISBN/EAN: 9783741157332

Manufactured in Europe, USA, Canada, Australia, Japa

Cover: Foto ©Andreas Hilbeck / pixelio.de

Manufactured and distributed by brebook publishing software (www.brebook.com)

Robert Williams Buchanan, Dalziel Brothers

North Coast And Other Poems

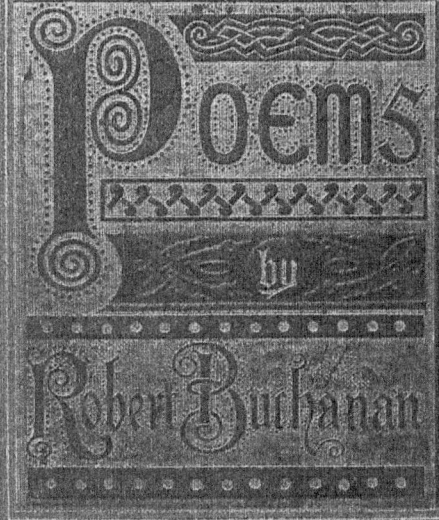

North Coast

and other

Poems

by

Robert Buchanan

So still, he noted not the dreamy stranger,
Who, breathing hard after the steep ascent,
Stood close at hand, and strangely looked upon him.

The Exiles of Osuna.—p. 179.

NORTH COAST

AND OTHER

POEMS

BY

ROBERT BUCHANAN

WITH ILLUSTRATIONS

BY

J. WOLF	A. B. HOUGHTON	W. SMALL
T. DALZIEL	G. J. PINWELL	E. DALZIEL
	J. B. ZWECKER,	

Engraved by the Brothers Dalziel

LONDON

GEORGE ROUTLEDGE AND SONS

THE BROADWAY, LUDGATE

NEW YORK: 416 BROOME STREET

1868

ANNOUNCEMENT.

THREE Poems in this volume have appeared before—'The Northern Muse,' 'An English Eclogue,' and 'A Scottish Eclogue;' all the others are now published for the first time.

Camden Press, October, 1867.

CONTENTS.

LIST OF ILLUSTRATIONS.

—◆—

NORTH COAST

AND OTHER

POEMS.

MEG BLANE.

(NORTH COAST, 18—.)

' L ORD, hearken to me!
    Help all poor men at sea!
Thy breath is on their cheeks,—
Their cheeks are wan wi' fear;
    Nae man speaks,
For wha could hear?
The long-haired sea-wives scream,
    The wind cries loud;
Ghaistly the fireflaughts gleam

On tattered sail and shroud;
Under the red mast-light
The hissing waters slip;
Thick reeks the storm o' night
Round him that steers the ship,
And his een are blind,
And he kens not where they run.
LORD, be kind!
Whistle back Thy wind,
For the sake of CHRIST Thy Son.'

And as she prayed she knelt not on her knee,
But, standing on the threshold, looked to sea;
Yet all was blackness and a watery roar,
Save when the red light, glistening far away,
Ghastlied the line of foam upon the shore,
And showed the ribbéd reef and surfy bay.
There was no sign of life across the dark,
No piteous light from fishing-boat or bark,
Albeit for such she listed so to pray.
With tattered plaid wrapt tight around her form,
She stood a space, blown on by wind and rain;
Then, sighing deep, she turnéd from the storm,
And crept into her lonely hut again.

It was a wooden hut under the height,
   Shielded in the black shadow of the crag:
One blow of such a wind as blew that night

Could rend so rude a dwelling like a rag;
But, gathering in the crannies overhead,
Down fell the spouting rain heavy as lead,
  So that the old walls and the rafters thin
Drippéd and steaméd, gloaming in the surf,
And the black rain-drops through the roof of turf
  Splashed momently on the mud floor within.
There, swinging from the roof, an earthen lamp
Waved to the wind and glimmered in the damp,
  And made strange shadows round the chamber bare
And on the household things of the poor place,
And glimmered faintly on the woman's face,
  Sooted with rain, and on her wringing hair.
    It was a piteous spot wherein to dwell,
    And yet she loved it well.

    'O mither, are ye there?'
A deep voice filled the dark, and she could hear.
  With hard hand she pushed back her dripping hair,
And kissed him. 'Whisht, my bairn, for mither's near.'
  Then on the shuttle bed a figure thin
    Sat rubbing sleeping eyes:
  A bearded man, with heavy hanging chin,
    And on his face a light not over-wise.

'Water!' he said; and deep his thirst was quelled
Out of the broken pitcher she upheld,
And yawning sleepily, he gazed around,
And stretched his limbs again, and soon slept sound.
Stooping, she smoothed his pillow 'neath his head,
  Still gazing down with eyes dewy and mild,
And while she gazed, softly he slumberéd,
      That bearded man, her child.
And a child's dreams were his; for as he lay,
He uttered happy cries as if at play,
And his strong hand was lifted up on high,
In act to catch the bird or butterfly;
And often to his bearded lips there came
      That lonely woman's name;
And though the storm of ocean roared so near,
      That one sweet word
      Was all the woman heard,
      And all she cared to hear.

Not old in years, though youth had passed away,
And the meek hair was tinged with silver gray,
Close to the gloaming of the day of life,
She stood, calm featured like a wedded wife;
And yet no wedded wife was she, but one

Whose foot had left the pathways of the just,
And meekly, since her penance had been done,
  Her true eyes sought men's faces, not the dust.
Her tearful days were over: she had found
Firm footing, work to do upon the ground;
The elements had welded her at length
      To their own truth and strength.

This woman was no slight and tear-strung thing,
Whose easy tears fall sweet on suffering,
But one in whom no stranger's eyes would seek
      For pity mild and meek.
Man's height was hers—man's strength and will thereto,
    Her shoulders broad, her step man-like and long;
'Mong fishermen she dwelt, a rude, rough crew,
    And more than one had found her fist was strong.
And yet her face was gentle, though the sun
      Had made it dark and dun;
      Her silver-threaded hair ·
Was combed behind her ears with cleanly care;
And she had eyes liquid and sorrow-fraught,
    And round her mouth were delicate lines that told
She was a woman sweet with her own thought,
    Though built upon a large, heroic mould.

Who did not know Meg Blane?
What hearth but heard the deeds that Meg had done?
What fisher of the main
But knew her, and her little-witted son?
For in the fiercest waters of the coast
Her black boat hovered and her net was tost,
And lonely in the watery solitude
The son and mother fished for daily food.
When on calm nights the herring hosts went by,
  Her black boat followed the red smacks from shore,
And smoking in the stern the man would lie
  While Meg was hoisting sail or plying oar;

Till, a black speck against the morning sky
  The boat came homeward, with its silver store.
And Meg was cunning in the ways of things,
  And watched what every changing lineament
  Of wind and sea and cloud and water meant,
Knowing how Nature threatens ere she springs.
  She knew the clouds as shepherds know their sheep,
To eyes unskilled alike, yet different each;
  She knew the wondrous voices of the deep;
The tones of sea-birds were to her a speech.
  Much faith was hers in GOD, who was her Guide;
Courage was hers such as GOD gives to few,
  For she could face His terrors fearless-eyed,
Yet keep the still weird woman's nature true.
  Lives had she snatched out of the waste by night,
      When stormy winds were blowing,
  And to sick-beds her presence carried light,
  When like a thin sail lessening out of sight
Some rude, rough life to the unknown sea was going;
  For he who scorned a feeble woman's wail
Would hear to one so strong and brave as she,
  Whose face had braved the lightning and the gale,
      And scarce grown pale,
Save when it looked on other lives at sea.

Yet often, as she lay a-sleeping there,
  She started up, blushing as if in shame,
And stretched out arms embracing the thin air,
    And named an unknown name;
And there was a strange listening in her face
  If sudden footsteps sounded in her ear;
And when strange seamen came unto the place
  She read their faces in a quiet fear;
And finding not the object of her quest,
  Her hand she pressèd hard upon her breast,
And wore a white look, and drew feeble breath,
    Like one that hungereth.

It was a night of summer, yet the wind
  Had wafted from the hills the rain-clouds dank,
Blown out heaven's thousand eyes and made it blind,
Though now and then the moon gleamed moist behind
  The rack, till, smitten by the drift, she sank.
    But the deep roared;
Sucked to the black cloud, spumed the foamy main,
  While lightning rent the storm-rack like a sword,
And earthward rolled the gray smoke of the rain.

'T is late, and yet the woman doth not rest,
But sitteth with chin drooping on her breast:

2

Weary she is, yet will not take repose;
Tiréd her eyes, and yet they cannot close;
She rocketh to and fro upon her chair,
          And stareth at the air.

Far, far away her thoughts were travelling:
     They could not rest—they wandered far and fleet,
Like wild white birds that o'er the waters wing,
     And cannot find a place to rest their feet;
And in her ear a thin voice murmuréd,
          'If he be dead—be dead!'
Then, even then, the woman's face went white
     And awful, and her eyes were fixed in fear,
For suddenly all the wild cries of night
     Were hushed: the wind lay down, and she could hear
Strange voices gather round her in the gloom,
Sounds of invisible feet across the room,
     And after that the rustle of a shroud,
          And then a creaking door,
     And last the coronach, full shrill and loud,
Of women clapping hands and weeping sore.

Then Meg knew well that ill was close at hand,
          On water or on land,

Because the glamour touched her lids like breath,
  And burned her heart; but in a waking swoon
Quiet she stayed,—not stirring,—cold as death,
      And heard those voices croon;
Then suddenly she heard a human shout,

The hurried falling of a foot without,
Then a hoarse voice—a knocking at the door—
    'Meg, Meg! a ship ashore!'

Now mark the woman! She has risen her height,
Her dripping plaid is wrapt around her tight;

Tight clenchéd in her palm her fingers are;
Her eye is steadfast as a fixéd star.
One look upon her child—he sleepeth on—
One step unto the door, and she is gone:
Barefooted out into the dark she fares,
   And comes where, rubbing eyelids thick with sleep,
The half-clad fishers mingle oaths and prayers,
       And look upon the deep.

      Black was the oozy lift,
      Black was the sea and land;
Hither and thither, thick with foam and drift,
     Did the deep waters shift,
  Swinging with iron clash on rock and sand.
Faintlier the heavy rain was falling,
Faintlier, faintlier the wind was calling
  With hollower echoes up the drifting dark,
And the swift rockets shooting through the night
Ghastlied the foamy reef with pale blue light,
  And showed the piteous outline of the bark
Rising and falling like a living thing,
      Shuddering, shivering,
While, howling beast-like, the white waters there
Spat blindness in the dank eyes of despair.

Then one cried, 'She has sunk!' and on the shore
Men shook, and on the heights the women cried;

But, lo! the outline of the bark once more!
  While blue and faint the rocket rose and died.
Ah, GOD, put out Thy hand! all for the sake
Of little ones, and weary hearts that wake!
  Be gentle! chain the fierce waves with a chain!
Let the gaunt seaman's little boys and girls
Sit on his knee and play with his black curls
        Yet once again!
And breathe the pale lad safely through the foam,
Back to the hungry mother in her home!
And spare the bad man, with his glazéd eye;
Kiss him, for CHRIST's sake, bid Thy Death go by—
        He hath no heart to die!

Now faintlier blew the wind, the thin rain ceased,
  The thick cloud cleared like smoke from off the strand,
For, lo! a faint blue glimmer in the east,—
        GOD putting out His hand!
And overhead the storm-rack thinnéd too,
        And through the smoky gorge
The wind drove past the stars, and faint they flew
        Like sparks blown from a forge;
And now the thousand foamy eyes o' the sea
        Hither and thither glimmered visibly,

And gray lights hither and thither travelléd,
Like dim shapes searching for the drownéd dead;
And where these shapes most thickly glamoured by,
　Out on the ribbéd reef the black hulk lay,
And cast, against the glimmering eastern sky,
　Its shape gigantic on the falling spray.

Yet there upon the shore the fishers fed
　Their eyes on horror, waiting for the close,
　　When sudden in the midst a shrill voice rose;
　　　'The boat! the boat!' it said.
Like creatures startled from a trance, they turned
　To her who spake: tall in the midst stood she,
With arms uplifted, and with eyes that yearned
　　　Out on the murmuring sea.
Some, shrugging shoulders, homeward turned their eyes,
　And others answered back in brutal speech;
But some, brave hearted, uttering shouts and cries,
　Followed the fearless woman up the beach.
A rush to seaward—black confusion—then
　A struggle with the sea upon the strand—
'Mid shrieks of women, cries of desperate men,
　The long oars smite, the black boat springs from land.
　　　Around the thick spray flies;

The waves roll round and seem to overwhelm.
  With blowing hair and onward-gazing eyes
The woman stands erect, and grips the helm. . . . .

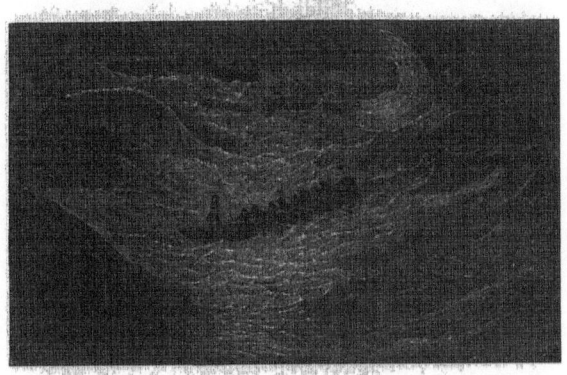

Now fearless heart, Meg Blane, or all must die!
Let not the skilled hand thwart the steadfast eye!
The ridgéd wave comes near,—crag-like it towers
Above ye, scattering round its foamy showers:
One flutter of the hand, and all is done!
Now steel thy heart, thou woman-hearted one!
      Softly the good helm guides;
Round to the ridgéd waves the boat leaps light,—

Hidden an instant,—on the foamy height,
  Dripping and quivering like a sea-bird, rides.
Now through the ragged rift the moon looms pale,
    Driven before the gale,
And makes a silver trouble with her breath,
Till duskily the water shimmereth;
And, lo! she gleameth on the reef, and on
  The black hull, as the fisher-boat comes nigh.
A crash!—the wreck upon the reef is gone!
  A scream!—and all is still beneath the sky,
  Save the weird waters as they foam and cry.

II.

DAWN; and the deep was still. Without her door,
     Meg, shading eyes against the morning sun,
Gazed seaward. After trouble there was peace.
Smooth, many-coloured, as a ring-dove's neck,
Stretchéd the deep, and on its eastern rim
The cool, sweet light, with rainy yellow beams,
Gleamed like a sapphire. Overhead, soft airs
To feathery cirrhus flecked the deepening blue;
Beneath, the smooth sea's breathing made a breeze;
And up the weedy beach the blue waves crept,
Breaking in one thin line of creamy foam.

Seaward the woman gazed, with keen eye fixed
On a dark shape that floated on the calm,
Drifting as seaweed; still and black it lay,
The outline of a lifeless human shape:
And yet it was no drownéd mariner,
For she who looked was smiling, and her face
Looked merry; and more merry when a boat,
With pale and timorous fishermen, drew nigh;
And as the fearful fishers paused and gazed,
A boat's length distant, leaning on their oars,
The shape took life—raised up a dripping head,
Screaming—flung up its body in white foam,
And, with a laugh they echoed with a curse,
Dived headlong, as a monster of the deep
Plunges deep down when startled on its couch
Of glassy waters. 'T was the woman's child,
The witless water-haunter—Angus Blane.

For Angus Blane, not fearless as the wise
Are fearless, loved the waters like a thing
Born in their still depths of the slimy ooze.
A child, he sported on their rim, and crept
Splashing with little hands amid the foam;
And when his limbs were stronger, and he reached

A young man's stature, the old sea had grown
Dear and familiar as his mother's face.
Far out he swam, on windless summer days,
Floating like some sea-monster far from land,
Plunging from terror-stricken fishermen,
With eldritch cry and wild unearthly face;
And in the untrodden deeps below the sea,
Awaking wondrous echoes, that had slept
Since first the watery Spirit stirred and breathed.
On summer gloamings, in the bay for hours
He glistened like a sea-snake in the moon,
Splashing with trail of glistening phosphor-fire,
And laughing shrill till echo answeréd,
And the pale helmsman on the passing boat,
Thinking some demon of the waters cried,
Shivered and prayed. His playmates were the waves,
The sea his playground. On his ear were sounds
Kinder than human voices; on his soul,
Though misted with his witless thoughts, there passed
A motion and a glamour that at times
Broke through his lips, and troubled witless words
With weird sea-music. When he was a child
Children had mocked him—he had shunned their sports,
And haunted ocean places,—nurturing

The bright, fierce, animal splendour of a soul
That ne'er was clouded through the pensive mists
Of mind that smoke the souls of wiser men.
Only in winter seasons he was sad;
For then the loving Spirit of the Deep
Repulsed him, and its smile was kind no more;
And on the strand he wandered; from deep caves
Gazed at the tempest; and from day to day
Moaned to his mother for the happy time
When the white swallows glisten from the South,
And summer glimmers through the rain, and brings
Smiles and a windless silence to the sea.

And as the deepening of strange melody,
Caught from the unknown shores beyond the seas,
Was the outspreading of his life to her
Who bare him; yea, at times, the woman's womb
Seemed laden with the throes of him unborn,
So close his being clave unto her flesh,
So strangely linked his spirit with her own.
For the forebodings of her heart, when first
She saw the mind-mists in his infant eyes,
And knew him witless, turned as years went on
Into more spiritual, mysterious love

Than common mothers feel; and he had power
To make her nature deeper, more alive
Unto the spiritual feet that walk
Our dark and troubled waters. Thence was born
Much of her courage on the sea, her trust
In the sea's MASTER; thence, moreover, grew
Her faith in visions, warnings, fantasies,
Such as came thronging on her heart when most
Her eyes looked inward—to the place wherein
She hid a secret sorrow.

                         While she gazed,
Smiling, the bearded face of Angus rose
Nearer to shore, and panting in the sun,
Laughed at the fishers. Then the woman turned,
And took, with man-like step and slow, a path
That, creeping through the shadows of the cliffs,
Wound to the clachan. In the clear, bright dawn
Lay Thornock glittering, while, thin and blue,
Curled peat-smoke from the line of fisher-huts
That parted the high shingle from the land.
The sea was low; amid the tangled weeds
And many-coloured rocks and sparkling pools,
Went stooping men and women, seeking spoil,

Treasure or drift-wood floating from the wreck;
Beyond, some stood in fish-boats, peering down,
Seeking the drownéd dead; and, near at hand,
So near, a tall man might have waded thither
With a dry beard, the reef loomed black with weed,

And there the sea-fowl ever and anon
Rose like a cloud of foam, whirled in the air,
And, screaming, settled. But not thitherward
Wandered Meg Blane. Along the huts she went—
Among the rainy pools where, shouting, played
Brown and barefooted bairns—among the nets

Stretched steaming in the sun—until she reached
The cottage she was seeking. At the door,
Smoking his pipe, a grizzly fisher sat,
Looking to sea. With him she spake awhile,
Then, with a troubled look, entered the hut,
And sought the inner chamber.

                                   Faint and pale
Light glimmered through a loop-hole in the wall,
A deep white streak across the rush-strewn floor,
All else in shadow; and the room was still,
Save for a heavy breathing, as of one
In quiet sleep. Within the wall's recess,
On the rude bed of straw the sleeper lay,
His head upon his arm, the sick thin light
Touching his upturned face; while Meg drew near,
And gazed upon him with a stranger's eyes,
Quiet and pitying. Though his sleep was sound,
His dreams were troubled. Throwing up his arms,
He seemed to beckon, muttering; then his teeth
Clenched tight, a white smile wrinkled on his brow,
And still he lay like one awaiting doom;
But suddenly, in agony supreme,
He breathed like one who struggles, sinks, and drowns.

Struggling, with wavering arms and quivering limbs,
And screaming in his throat, he fought for life;
Till, half-awakening with the agony,
His glazéd eyes he oped and glaréd round,
While Meg drew shivering back into the shade;
And then, with deeper breath, as if relieved,
Dropped down his bearded face upon his arm,
And slept again.

           Then Meg stole stilly forth,
And in the outer chamber found a lamp,
And lit the same in silence, and returned
On tiptoe to the sleeper. As she went,
White as a murdered woman's grew her face,
Her mouth was clenchéd as in death; her eyes
With ring on ring of widening wonder glared,
Fixéd to fascination upon him
Who slumbered. Closer still she crept,
Holding the lamp aloft, until his breath
Was hot upon her cheek,—so gaunt, so white,
It seemed her time was come. Yet in her look
Was famine. As one famished looks on food
After long agony, and thinks it dream,
She gazed and gazed, nor stirred, nor breathed, nor lived,

4

Save in her spirit's hunger gleaming forth
Out of her eyes; till suddenly the man,
Half-opening his eyes, reached out his arms
And gript her, crying, 'Silence! pray to GOD!
She's sinking!' and, with shrill and eldritch groan,
Awakened.
                    Then the woman would have fled
Had he not gript her. In her face he gazed,
Thrusting one hand into his silvered hair,
And sought to gather close his scattered thoughts.
And his eye brightened, and he murmured low,
'Where am I? Dead or living? Ah, I live!
The ship? the ship?' Meg answered not, but shrank
Into the shadow; till she saw the mists
Pass from his bearded face and leave it clear,
And heard his voice grow calmer, measuréd
By tranquil heart-beats. Then he asked again,
'The ship? How many live of those aboard?'
And when she answered he alone was saved,
He groaned; but with a sailor's fearless look,
'Thank GOD for that,' he said; 'and yet He might
Have spared a better man. Where am I, friend?'
'On the north coast,' said Meg, 'upon the shore
At Thornock.'

Could the seaman, while she spake,
Have marked the wondering light on that pale face,

All else,—the storm, the terrible fight with death,—
Had been forgotten; but his glazéd eye
Saw dimly. Grasping still her quivering wrist,
He questioned on; and, summoning strength of heart,
In her rude speech she told him of the storm:
How to the watery gulf the ship had rolled
When aid was nigh; how, hovering near its tomb,
The fishers from the whirling waters dragged
Two drownéd seamen and himself, a corpse
In seeming; how by slow and gentle means
They wound his thin and bloody thread of life
Out of the slowly-loosening hands of Death.

III.

Then, with strange trouble in her eyes, Meg Blane
Crept swiftly back unto her hut again,
Like one that fleeth from some fearful thing;
Then sat and made a darkness, covering
Her face with apron old, and thought apart;
And yet she scarce could think, for ache of heart,
But saw dead women and dead men go by,

And felt the wind, and heard the waters cry,
And on the waters, as they washed to shore,
Saw one Face float alone and glimmer hoar
Through the green darkness of the breaking brine.

And Meg was troubled deep, nor could divine
The wherefore of her trouble, since 't was clear
The face long wishéd for at last was near,
Since all her waiting on was at an end.
Ay, Meg was dull, and could not comprehend
How GOD put out His breath that day, and blew
Her sailor to her feet before she knew,
And misted the dull future from her sight;
Wherefore she staréd down on her delight
As on a dead face washing in from sea.
But when she understood full certainlie
The thing had come according to her prayer,
Her strength came back upon her unaware,
And she thanked GOD, albeit the pleasure seemed
Less absolute a bliss than she had dreamed
When it was a sweet trouble far away;
For she was conscious how her hair was gray,
Her features worn, her flesh's freshness gone,
Through toiling in the sun and waiting on;

And quietlie she murmured, weeping not,
'Perchance—for men forget—he hath forgot.'

And two long days she was too dazed and weak
To step across the sands to him, and speak;
But on the third day, pale with her intent,
She took the great hand of her son, and went,
Not heeding while the little-witted one
Mouthed at the sea and muttered in the sun;
And firmly stepping on along the shore,
Beheld afar off, at the cottage door,
The figure of her shipwrecked marinere;
When, deeply troubled by a nameless fear,
She lingered o'er her footsteps, pale and wan.

Then, coming near, she noted how the man
Sat sickly, holding out his arm to please
A fisher bairn he held between his knees,
Whose eyes looked on the mighty arm and bare,
Where ships, strange faces, anchors, pictured were,
Pricked blue into the skin with many a stain;
And, sharply marking the man's face, Meg Blane
Was cheered and holpen, and she trembled less,
Thinking, 'His heart is full of kindliness.'

And, feeling that the thing if to be done
Must be done straight, she hastened with her son,
And, though she saw the man's shape growing dim,
Came up with feverish smile and spoke to him,
Pausing not, though she scarce could hear or see,
'Has Angus Macintyre forgotten me?'
And added quickly, 'I am Maggie Blane!'

Whereat the man was smit by sudden pain
And wonder—yea, the words he heard her speak
Were like a jet of fire upon his cheek;
And, rising up erect, 'Meg Blane!' he cried,
And, white and chilly, thrust the bairn aside,
And peered upon the woman all amazed,
While, pressing hard upon her heart, she gazed
Blankly at the dim mist she knew was he.

Then for a space both stood confusedlie,
In silence; but the man was first to gain
Calmness to think and power to speak again;
And, though his bloodless lips were pressèd tight,
Into his eyes he forced a feeble light,
And took her shivering hand, and named her name
In forced kind tones, yet with a secret shame,
Nor sought to greet her more with touch or kiss.

But she, who had waited on so long for this,
Feeling her hand between his fingers rest,
Could bear no more, but fell upon his breast,
Sobbing and moaning like a little bairn.

Then, while her arms were round him, he looked stern,
With an unwelcome burden ill at ease,
What time she freed her heart in words like these—
'At last! at last! O Angus, let me greet!
God's good! I never hoped that we would meet!
Lang, lang hae I been waiting by the sea,
Waiting and waiting, praying on my knee;
And God said I should look again on you,
And, though I daredna hope, God's word comes true,
And He hath put an end to my distress!'
And, as she spoke, her child plucked at her dress,
Made fierce grimaces at the man, and tried
To draw her from the breast whereon she cried;
But looking up, she pointed to her child,
And gazed full piteous at the man, and smiled.
'God help him, Angus! 'T is the bairn!' she said;—
Nor noted how the man grew shamed and red,
With child and mother ill at ease and wroth,
And wishing he were many a mile from both.

5

For now Meg's heart was many a mile away,
And unto her it seemed but yesterday
That, standing inland in a heathery dell,
At dead o' night, she bade the man farewell,
And heard him swear full fondly in her ear
Sooner or late to come with gold and gear,
And marry her in kirk by holy rite;
And at the memory a quiet light,
Rose-like and maiden, came upon her face,
And softened her tall shape to nameless grace,
As low winds blowing on a birk-tree green
Make it one rippling trouble of white sheen.

But soon from that remembrance driven again
By the man's silence and his pallid pain,
She shivered for a moment as with cold,
And left his bosom, looking grieved and old,
Yet smiling, forcing a sweet smile, and seeking
For tokens in his face more sweet than speaking.

But he was dumb, and with a pallid frown,
Twitching his fingers quick, was looking down.
'What ails thee, Angus?' cried the woman, reading
His face with one sharp look of interceding;

Then, looking downward too, standing apart,
With blood like water slipping through her heart,
Because she thought, ' 'T is ill if it should be
That Angus cares no more for mine and me,
Since I am old and worn with sharp distress,
And men like pretty looks and daintiness ;
And since we parted twenty years have past,
And that, indeed, is long for a man's heart to last.'

But, agonized with looking at her woe,
And bent to end her hope with one sharp blow,
The troubled man, uplifting hands, spake thus,
In rapid accents, sharp and tremulous :
' Too late, Meg Blane ! seven years ago I wed
Another woman, thinking you were dead,— ··
And I have bairns !' And there he paused, for fear.

As when, with ghostly voices in her ear,
While in her soul, as in a little well,
The dusky silver of the glamour fell,
She had been wont to hark o' nights alone,
So stood she now, not stirring, still as stone,
While in her soul, with desolate refrain,
The words, ' Too late !' rang o'er and o'er again ;

And gazéd on his face with chill white stare;
Then raising her wild arms into the air,
Pinching her face together in sharp fear,
She quivered to the ground without a tear,
And put her face into her hands, and thrust
Her hair between her teeth, and spat it forth like dust.

And though, with pity in his guilty heart,
The man spake on and sought to heal her smart,

She heard not, but was dumb and deaf in woe;
But when, in pain to see her grieving so,
Her son put down his hand, and named her name,
And whispered, 'Mither! mither! let us hame!'
She gript the hand, and smoothed her features wan,
And rose erect, not looking at the man,
But, gazing down, moved slowly from the spot.

Over this agony I linger not,
Nor shall I picture how upon that shore
They met and spoke and parted yet once more,
So calmly that the woman understood
Her hope indeed had gone away for good.
But ere the man departed from the place
It seemed to Meg, contemplating his face,
Her love for him had ne'er been so intense
As it had seemed when he was far from thence;
And many a thing in him seemed little-hearted
And mean and loveless; so that ere they parted
She seemed unto her sorrow reconciled.
And when he went away, she almost smiled,
But bitterlie, and turned to toil again,
And felt most hard to all the world of men.

IV.

LORD, with how small a thing
Thou canst prop up the heart against the grave!
       A little glimmering
          Is all we crave;
        The coming of a love
          That hath no being;
   The thin point of a little star above,
          Flashing and fleeing,
        Contents our seeing.
The house that never will be built; the gold
        That never will be told;
The task we leave undone when we are cold;
The dear face that returns not, but is lying,
   Licked by the leopard, in an Indian cave;
The coming rest that cometh not, till, sighing,
   We turn our weary eyes upon the grave.
        And, LORD, how should we dare
          Thither in peace to fall,

But for a feeble glimmering even there—
Falsest, perchance, of all?
We are as children in Thy hands indeed,
And Thou hast easy comfort for our need,—
The shining of a lamp, the tinkling of a bell,
Content us well.

And even when Thou bringest to our eyes
A little thing, to show its worthlessness,
Anon we see another thing arise,
And we are comforted in our distress;
And, waiting on, we watch it glittering,
Till in its turn it is a worthless thing;
And even as we weep
Another rises, and we smile again;
Till, wearied out with watching on in vain,
We fall to sleep.

And often one poor light that looks divine
Is all one soul seeketh along the ground;
There are no more to shine
When that one thing is found.
If it be worthless, then what shall suffice?
The lean hand grips a speck that was a spark,

The heart is turned to ice,
    And all the world is dark.
Hard are Thy ways when that one thing is brought
    Close, touched, and proven nought.
Far off it is a mighty spell, and strong
        To help a life along.
But, lo! it darkens hitherward, and now
    Droppeth, a rayless stone, upon the sod.—
The world is lost: perchance not even Thou
        Survivest it, LORD GOD!

    In poverty, in pain,
    For weary years and long,
One hope, one fear, had comforted Meg Blane,
    Yea, made her brave and strong;
A hope so faint, it seemed not hope at all,
    But a sweet trouble and a dreamy fear,
A hearkening for a voice, a soft footfall,
    She never hoped in sober heart to hear:
        This had been all her cheer;
            And with this balm
            Her soul might have kept calm
        For many another year.
        In terror and in desolation, she

Had been sustained,
And never felt abandoned utterly
While that remained.
LORD, in how small and poor a space can hide
The motives of our terror and our pride,
The clue unto the fortunate man's distress,
The secret of the hero's fearlessness!
What had sustained this woman on the sea
When strong men turned to flee?
Not courage, not despair,
Not pride, not household care,
Not faith in Thee!
Nought but a hungry instinct blind and dim—
A fear, a nameless pain,
A dreamy wish to gaze again on him
She never wholly hoped to see again.

Nor all at once,—nor in an hour, a day,
Did the strong woman feel her force depart,
Or know how utterly had passed away
The meaning of her heart;
It was not love she missed, for love was dead,
And surely had been dead long ere she knew;
She did not miss the man's face when it fled,

6

As passionate women do:
She saw him turn into the world again,
        And had no pain;
And shook him by the hand, and watched him go,
        And thought it better so.
She turnéd to her task-work as of old,
Kissed her bearded child with love tenfold,
Hoisted the sails and plied the oar,
        And wandered out from shore,
        And for a little space
        Wore an unruffled face,
Though wind and water helped her heart no more.
But, mark: she knelt less often on her knees,
        For, labour as she might,
        By day or night,
She could not work enough to give her ease;
And presently her tongue, with sharper chimes,
        Chided at times.
And she who had endured such sharp distress
Grew peevish, flushing at her peevishness;
        And though she did not weep,
    Her features seemed with tears disfiguréd,
And in the night, when bitterest mourners sleep,
    She feverishly tossed upon her bed.

Slowly the trouble grew, and soon she found
  Less pleasure in the loud unrestful sea;
The wind and water had a duller sound,
    The moon and stars were sick as corpse-lights be;
Then more and more strange voices filled her ear,
      And ghostly feet came near,
And strange fire blew her eyelids down, and then
      Dead women and dead men,
Dripping with phosphor, rose, and, ere she wist,
      Went by in a cold mist;
Nor left her strengthenéd at heart and bold,
      As they had done of old;
  But ever after they had gone away
    She had no heart to pray.
    Bitter and dull and cold,
  She shivered back into the common day.

      Out of the east by night
        Drifted the black storm-cloud;
The air was hushed with snow-flakes falling white,
      But the seas below were loud;
    And out upon the reef the piteous light
      Rose from a shipwrecked bark
        Into the dark.

Pale stood the fishers, watching for the close,
Till suddenly the fearless cry arose,
And forth into the foam the black boat flew,
And fearless to their places leapt the crew.
Then one called out 'Meg Blane!'
　　But Meg stood by, and trembled and was dumb,
Till, smit unto the heart by sudden pain,
　　Into her hair she thrust her fingers numb,
　　　　And fell upon the sands,
And spake not while the wondering fishers called,
　　And tore the slippery seaweed with her hands,
　　　　And screamed, and was appalled.

And in that hour the woman's fearless strength
　　　　Snapt like a thread at length,
And tears, ev'n such as suffering women cry,
　　　　Fell from her eyes anon;
And she knew well, although she knew not why,
　　The charm she had against the deep was gone.
　　　　And after that dark hour,
　　　　She as a feeble shadow anguishéd.
　　　　All terrible things of power
　　　　Turned into things of dread,
And all the peace of all the world had fled.

Then only in still weather did she dare
  To seek her bread on ocean, as of old,
And in the stormy time her shelf was bare,

And her hearth black and cold;
Then very bitterly, with heart gone wild,
          She clung about her child,
And hated all the earth beneath the skies,
Because she saw the hunger in his eyes.

For on his mother's strength the witless wight
          Had leant for guide and light,
And food had ever come unto his hand,
     And he had known no thought of suffering;
Yea, all his life and breath on sea and land
          Had been an easy thing.
And now there was a change in his sole friend
          He could not comprehend.
But, lo! unto the shade of her distress
His nature shaped itself in gentleness;
And when he found her weeping, he too wept,
     And if she laughed, laughed out in company;
And often to the fisher-huts he crept,
     And begged her bread, and brought it tenderly,
And held it to her mouth, and till she ate
     Would touch no piece, although he hungered sore.
And these things were a solace to her fate,
     But wrung her heart the more.

Yea, to the bitter dolour of her days,
In witless mimicry he shaped his ways.
He fared but seldom now upon the sea,
   But wandered with his mother hand in hand,

Hunting for faggots on the inland lea,
   Or picking dulse for food upon the strand.
Something had made the world more sad and strange,
But easily he changéd with the change.

For in the very trick of woe he clad
His features, and was sad since she was sad,
And leant his chin upon his hands like her,
    And looked at vacancy; and when the deep
    Was troublous, and she started up from sleep,
He too awoke, with fearful heart astir;
And aye the more her bitter tears she shed
    Upon his neck, in woe to mark his woe,
The more in blind, deep love he fashionéd
    His grief to hers, and was contented so.

And as a tree inclineth, weak and bare,
Under an unseen weight of wintry air,
Beneath her load the weary woman bent,
And, stooping double, trembled as she went;
And the days snowed their snows upon her head
       As they went by,
       And ere a year had fled
       She felt that she must die.

Then like a thing whom very witlessness
    Maketh indifferent, she lingered on,
Not caring to abide with her distress,
       Not caring to be gone;

But gazing with a dull and fixéd eye,
  And seeing dreams pass by;
Not speculating whither she would go,
But feeling there was nought she cared to know,
  And melting even as snow.
Save when the man's hand slipped into her own,
  And fluttered fondly there,
And she would feel her life again, and groan,
' My God! when I am gone, how will he fare?'
  And for a little time, for Angus' sake,
   Her bruiséd heart would ache,
  And all life's stir and anguish once again
   Would swoon across her brain.

  ' O bairn, when I am dead,
   How shall ye keep frae harm?
  What hand will gie ye bread?
   What fire will keep ye warm?
How shall ye dwell on earth awa' frae me?'—
   ' O mither, dinna dee!'

  ' O bairn, by night or day
   I hear nae sounds ava',
   But voices o' winds that blaw,

7

And the voices o' ghaists that say
I must awa'.
The Lord that made the wind, and made the sea,
Is hard on my bairn and me,
And I melt in His breath like snaw.'—
'O mither, dinna dee!'

'O bairn, it is but closing up the een,
And lying down never to rise again.
Many a strong man's sleeping hae I seen,—
There is nae pain!
I 'm weary, weary, and I kenna why;
My summer has gone by,
And sweet were sleep, but for the sake o' thee.'—
'O mither, dinna dee!'

But when sweet summer scents were on the sea,
And 'neath the moon the waves plashed bright and
cool,
Outside the hut she sat upon a stool,
While Angus leant his head against her knee,
And with thin fingers fashioned carefully
A long white dress of wool.
'O mither,' cried the man, 'what make ye there?'

' A blanket for our bed !'
' O mither, it is like the sark folk wear
   When they are drowned and dead !'

And Meg said nought, but kissed him on the lips,
   And looked with dull eye seaward, where the moon
Silvered the white sails of the passing ships,
   Into the land where she was going so soon.

And in the reaping-time she lay abed,
And by her side the dress unfinishéd,
And with dull eyes that knew not even her child
She gazed at vacancy, and sometimes smiled;
And ever her fingers worked, for in her thought,
Stitching and stitching, still the dress she wrought;
And then a beldame old, with bleared ee,
Came to the hut for CHRIST and charitie,
And stilly sewed the woollen shroud herself,
And set the salt and candle on a shelf.
And like a dumb thing crouching moveless there,
  Gripping the fingers wan,
Marking the face with wild and wandering stare,
 And whining beast-like, watched the witless man.

 Then like a light upon a headland set,
In winds that came from far-off waters blowing,
 The faint life glimmered—fainter—fainter yet;
But suddenly it brightened at its going;
And Meg sat up, and, lo! her features wore
The fearless sweetness they had known of yore;
And delicate lines were round her mouth; sweet rest
 Was in her eyes, though they were waxing dim;
And when the man crept close unto her breast,

She calmly kisséd him.
And it was clear
She had heard tidings it was sweet to hear,
And had no longer any care or fear.
' I gang, my bairnie, and ye will come to me !'
' O mither, dinna dee !'
But as he spake she dropped upon the bed,
And darkened, while the breath came thick and fleet :
' O Jessie, see they mind my bairn !' she said,
And quivered,—and was sleeping at GOD's feet.

When on her breast the plate of salt was laid,
And the corpse-candle burnt with sick blue light,
The man crouched, fascinated and afraid,
Beside her, whining through the night ;
And answered not the women who stole near,
And would not see nor hear ;
And when a day and night had come and gone,
Ate at the crusts they brought, and gazéd on ;
And when they took her out upon a bier,
He followed quietlie without a tear ;
And when upon the kist fell dust and stone,
He murmured a thin answer to the sound,
And at the end he sat, with a dull moan,

        Upon the new-made mound.

And as a dog that mourns a master dead,
   The man did haunt the grave in dull dumb pain;
Creeping away to beg a little bread,
        Then stealing back again;
And he was held accursed who did not give
The gift of bread or meal, that he might live;—
        Till, dull and piteous-eyed,
He moaned beneath a load too hard to bear.
        'Mither!' he cried,—
And crawled into the dark, to seek her there.

A PRELUDE.

O THOU whose ears incline unto my singing,
  Turn with me to the mountains, and behold
A sad thing in the land wherein thou dwellest.

I have to utter dread things of man's heart;
I have to point at evil with my finger;
I have to find the light of GOD in evil.

And yet I am no wielder of the thunders;
I have no little curse to hurl at sinners:
My full heart hungers out unto the stainéd.

I have a word to leave upon my tombstone;
I have a token for the men who follow:—
' *This man's heart hungered out unto the stainéd.*'

And love and sorrow and wrong shall scent my song;
From discords I will wring harmonious breathings,
Sounding a plea for all men, here and yonder.

For I have stains upon me, and am base:
It is not much that such a man can say;
And yet 't is much, if said with all his might.

II.

O thou whose ears incline unto my singing,
Woman or man, thou surely bear'st thy burden,
And I who sing, and all men, bear their burdens.

Even as a meteor-stone from suns afar,
Didst thou not reach the ways of life, and breathe?
No wonder that to much thou art a stranger.

Sweet, sweet it is to sit in leafy places,
In a green darkness, and to hear the stirring
Of strange breaths hither—thither—in the branches;

And sweet it is to sail on purple waters,
Between the heaven o'er and heaven under,
The hills above us, and their ghosts beneath us;

And sweet it is to watch the blue-maned lightning
Spring shrieking at the earth, and slowly perish
Under the falling of the leaden rain.

Thou lov'st all grand and gentle and sweet things,—
The wind-flower at the tree-root, and the white cloud,
The strength of mountains, and the power of waters.

And unto thee all seasons utter pleasure :
Spring, standing startled, listening to the skylark,
The wild flowers from her lap unheeded falling;

And Summer, in her gorgeous loose apparel;
And Autumn, with her dreamy silver eyebrows;
And Winter, with his white hair blown about him.

Yea, everywhere there stirs a dreamy beauty,
A gleaming and a flashing unto change,
An under-stream of sober meditation.

Yet nought endures, but all their glory fadeth,
And power and sweet and sorrow are interwoven;
There is no single presence of the Godhead.

8

III.

The world is wondrous round thee — Go<small>D</small>'s green
    world—
A world of pleasant waters and soft places,
And weirdly woven colours in the air.

Yet evermore a trouble doth pursue thee,—
A hunger for the wherefore of thy being,
A wonder from what regions thou hast fallen.

Thou gladdenest in the glad things of the world,
Yet criest surely, ' Wherefore, and oh, wherefore ?
What am I ? wherefore doth the world seem happy ?'

Thou saddenest in the sad things of the world,
Yet criest on, ' Why are men bruised and beaten ?
Whence do I grieve and gladden to no end ?'

Thy trouble grows tenfold when thou beholdest
The agony and burden of thy fellows,
The pains of sick men, and the groans of hungry.

Thou seest the good man tear his hair and weep;
Thou seest the bad man tread on human necks,
Prospering and blaspheming; and thou wonderest.

The silken-natured woman is a bond-slave;
The gross man fouls her likeness in high places;
The innocent are heart-wrung; and thou wonderest.

The gifts of earth are given to the base;
The monster of the cities spurns the martyr;
The martyr dies, denying; and thou wonderest.

How shalt thou reconcile these bitter things?
How shalt thou cast thy hope beyond the sunset?
The sweetest man's conception is a coward's.—

How shalt thou ask for more from him who singeth?
He can but sing aloud that these things are,
And look about for signs that God perceives them.

IV.

The singer is the curious-eyéd man
Who searches in the byeways of the world
For little signs the LORD has dropped in passing.

For where His robe has brushed grow grass and
    pansies,
And where His smile has fallen there are song birds,
And where His tears have dropped are tear-strung
    women ;

And from His strange mysterious robe, in passing,
Drop jewels, and they lie in gloomy places,—
Yea, in the dark depths of a murderer's spirit.

There is no place so wholly desolate
But tokens of His passing there lie hidden :
The curious-eyéd man must seek these out.

Have I not found them in an outcast's hair?
And in the breast and on the feet of sinners?
There is no place so base that God hath scorned it.

And ever, when he comes upon such tokens,
A glamour fills the vision of the singer,
And he is sure the Lord hath passed that way.

And 't is his task to put on blearéd eyes
The euphrasy of beauty, that his fellows
May see as he hath seen, and so be holpen.

There is no hope but one for him who singeth,—
To wander in the highways and the byeways,
To see deep down into the depths of action.

Is there a cheek on earth he would not kiss?
—Let him upon a mountain-top, and there
Ask for the lightning of annihilation.

v.

All is not o'er if loving is not o'er:
Somewhere the basest thing contacts with GOD;
The curious-eyéd man discovers where.

He sitteth not within a purple chamber;
He hath read deep in books and deep in souls;
The cunning of a craft is on his fingers.

He knoweth the dark windings up to GOD;
He goeth where the murderer's knife is lifted,
But feareth not.—GOD hath him by the hand.

He hath no stool to sit and suck his thoughts on;
He hath no creed where all creeds may not join him;
He hath no love that is not love for all men.

The eyes of men and women love the distant;
They scorn the wonders on their hearths and thresholds.
How should the stale grass on their doors look fair?

But, lo! the singer passeth by, and straightway
The common things are looming in the distance,
Distant in beauty and in revelation;

And long thin lines of meaning gleam afar off,
Like shafts of moonlight shimmering sweetly upward,
And then the singer's voice is heard intoning.

And evermore the singer's soul is troubled, ·
When Music, with her beautiful eyes bent upward,
Springs from his side, and soars, of earth disdainful.

And evermore, in those consummate moments,
The singer cries, 'GOD is above the world!
Up, up! sing in His ears, belovéd spirit.'

And o'er the wastes where weary eyes are watching,
A sudden glory is shaken, like a banner
Unfolded rapidly to strains of music.

AN ENGLISH ECLOGUE.

Timothy.

WELL, here's the cuckoo come again, after the
barley sowing,
The duckweed white upon the pond, all round the violets
blowing,
The gorse has got its coat of gold, and smells as sweet as
clover,
The lady-smocks are in the hedge, the primroses nigh
over,
And out upon the common there you see the lambkins
leaping,
The very snakes crawl here and there, — but Holy
Tommie's sleeping.

Jacob.

Ah, him that used to work with Bourne!   Bourne told
me how he blundered.

He used to preach.   I heard him once.   LORD! how he
   groaned and thundered!
The women squeaked like sucking-pigs, the men roared
   out like cattle,
And my gray hair stood up on end!

TIMOTHY.

               All ignorant stuff and tattle!
He lost his head through meddling so with things that
   don't concern us;
When we go questioning too close, 't is little GOD will
   learn us:
'T is hard enough to squeeze the crops from His dry
   ground about us,
But as for serving 't other world,—it gets its crops without
   us.
Ah, Tommie's was a loss that used to put me out com-
   pletely!
No man about could plough a field or kill a pig so neatly.

JACOB.

That's where it lies!   We get no good by asking ques-
   tions, neighbour:

Parsons are sent to watch our souls, while we are hard at labour:

9

This world needs help to get along, for men feed one
    another,
And what do we pay parsons for,—if not to manage
    't other ?

TIMOTHY.

You 're right ! No man as grumbles so with this here
    world has thriven ;
Mutton won't drop into our mouths, although we gape
    at heaven.
Why, Tommie was a ruddy lad, as rosy as an apple,
Till Methodism filled his head, and he was seen at chapel,
Found out that he 'd received a call, grew dismal, dull,
    and surly,
Read tracts when working in the fields, went praying late
    and early,
And by-and-bye began himself to argue with the
    doubting,
And though he 'd scarcely been to school, began his
    public spouting.
And soon I found—I wasn't blind—how he let matters
    go here,—
While he was at his heavenly work, things suffered down
    below here :

The hens dropped off through want of feed, horses grew
    sick and useless,
For lack o' milking presently the cows grew dry and
    juiceless;
And when I sought him out, and swore in rage and con-
    sternation,
I'm hanged if Tommy didn't cry and talk about salva-
    tion!
' Salvation's mighty well,' says I, right mad with my disaster,
' But since I want my farm-stock saved, you find another
    master!'
And I was firm, and sent him off, though he seemed
    broken-hearted:
He slipt a tract into my fist the morning he departed;
Ay, got a place next day with Bourne, who knew the lad
    was clever,
But dawdled still about his work, and preached as much
    as ever.

JACOB.

But Bourne soon sent him packing off—Bourne's just
    the sort of fellow;
Why, even when the parson calls, he grumbles and looks
    yellow!

TIMOTHY.

He got another master, though, but soon began to tire
    him ;

His wages sank, and by-and-bye no farmer here would
    hire him ;

And soon between this world and that, poor Tommie grew
    more mournful,

His strength and cleverness went off—the country folk
    looked scornful—

And 'soon the blessed Methodists grew tired, and would
    not hear him,

And bolted when he tried to speak, and shrank from sit-
    ting near him.

JACOB.

'T is just the way with Methodists. Give me the High
    Church, neighbour.

TIMOTHY.

' Why don't you be a man ?' said they, ' keep clean, and do
    your labour ?'

And what d' ye think that Tommie said ?—' I don't play
    shilly-shally ;

If I 'm to serve the LORD at all, 't will be continuálly :

You think that you can grub and cheat from Sunday on
to Sunday,

And put the LORD ALMIGHTY off by howling out on
one day ;

But if you want to get to heaven, your feelings must be
stronger.'

And Holy Tommie would not go to chapel any longer.

Learned sense ? No, no ! Reformed ? Not he ! But
moped and fretted blindly,

Because the blessed Methodists had used him so un-
kindly.

His life grew hard, his back grew bare, his brain grew
dreadful airy,

He thought of t' other world the more 'cause this seemed
so contrary ;

Went wandering on the river-side, and in the woods lay
lurking,

Gaped at the sky in summer-time when other men were
working,

And once was spied a-looking up where a wild lark was
winging,

And tears a-shining in his eyes,—because the lark was
singing !

Last harvest-time he came to me, and begged for work so
    sadly,

And vowed he had reformed so much, and looked so sick
    and badly,

I had not heart to send him off, but put him out
    a-reaping,

But, LORD! the same tale o'er again—he worked like
    one half-sleeping.

' Be off!' says I, ' you 're good for nought;' and all the rest
    stood sneering.

' Master, you may be right,' says he,—' the LORD seems
    hard o' hearing!

I thought I could fulfil below the call that I had
    gotten,

But here 's the harvest come again, and all my life seems
    rotten.

The Methodists are little good, the High Church folk
    are lazy,

And even when I pray alone, the ways o' Heaven seem
    hazy.

Religion don't appear to keep an honest lad from sad
    things,

And though the world is fine to see, 't is full of cruel bad
    things.

Why, I can't walk in fields and lanes, and see the flowers
a-growing,
And look upon the bright blue sky, or watch the river
flowing,
But even there, where things look fine, out creeps the
speckled adder,
Or silver snakes crawl by, and all at once the world looks
sadder.
The better I have seemed to grow, the worse all things
have gone with me.
It's all a great blank mystery! I wish the LORD was done
with me!"
And slowly, ever after that, Tommie grew paler, stiller,
And soon he could not work at all, and quickly he grew
iller :
And when the early new-year rains were yellowing pool
and river,
He closed his eyes, and slept, and gave the puzzle up for
ever.

JACOB.

His head was gone, that's clear enough—the chapel set
it turning.

TIMOTHY.

Now, this is how I look at it, although I have no learning :
In this here world, to do like him is nothing but self-
    slaughter,—
He went close to the edge o' life, and heard a roar like
    water,
His head went round, his face grew pale, his blood lost
    life and motion,—
'Twas just as vi'lets lose their scent when set beside the
    ocean.
But there's the parson riding up, with Doctor Barth, his
    crony ;
Some of these days the parson's weight will kill that
    blessed pony !
Ah, he 's the man to settle things that make the wits un-
    steady !
Wife, here 's the parson ! Draw some ale, and set the
    table ready.

THE BATTLE OF DRUMLIE-MOOR.

(NORTH COAST. COVENANT PERIOD.)

B AR the door! put out the light, for it gleams
  across the night,
And guides the bloody motion of their feet;
Hush the bairn upon thy breast, lest it guide them
 in their quest,
 And with water quench the blazing of the peat.
Now, wife, sit still and hark!—hold my hand amid
 the dark;
 O Jeanie, we are scattered e'en as sleet!

It was down on Drumliemoor, where it slopes upon
 the shore,
 And looks upon the white surf of the bay,
In the kirkyard of the dead, where the heather is
 turned red
 By the bloody clan that sleep beneath the clay;

10

And the Howiesons were there, and the people of
    Glen Ayr,
  And we gathered in the dark o' night to pray.

How! Sit at home in fear, when GOD's voice was
    in mine ear,
  When the priests of Baal were slaughtering His
    sheep?
Nay, there I took my stand, with my reap-hook in
    my hand,
  For bloody was the sheaf that I might reap;
And the LORD was in His skies, with a thousand
    dreadful eyes,
  And His breathing made a trouble on the deep.

Each mortal of the band brought his weapon in his
    hand,
  Though the chopper or the spit was all he bare;
And not a man but knew the work he had to do,
  If the Fiend should fall upon us unaware.
And our looks were ghastly white, but it was not
    with affright,
  For we knew the LORD was hearking to our
    prayer.

Oh, solemn, sad, and slow, rose the stern voice of
Monroe,

And he cursed the curse of Babylon the Whore;
And we could not see his face, but a gleam was in
    its place,
    Like the phosphor of the foam upon the shore;
And the eyes of all were dim as they fixed them-
    selves on him,
    And the Sea filled up the pauses with its roar.

And when, with accents calm, Kilmahoe gave out
    the psalm,
    And the sweetness of GOD's voice was on his
    tongue,
With one voice we praised the LORD of the Fire
    and of the Sword,
    And louder than the winter wind it rung;
And across the stars on high went the reek of
    vapour by,
    And a white mist drifted round us as we sung.

It was terrible to hear our cry rise deep and clear,
    Though we could not see the criers of the cry,
But we sang and gripped our brands, and touched
    each other's hands,
    While a thin sleet smote our faces from the sky;

And, sudden, strange, and low, hissed the accents of
    Monroe,
'Grip your weapons! Yea, be silent! They are
    nigh!'

And heark'ning, with clenched teeth, we could hear
    across the heath
The tramping of the horses as they flew,
And no man breathed a breath, but all were still
    as death,
And close together shivering we drew;

And deeper round us fell all the eyeless gloom of Hell,
    And the Fiend was in among us ere we knew.

Then a shriek of men arose, and the cursing of
    our foes—
    No face of friend or foeman could we mark ;
But I struck and kept my stand, trusting GOD to
    guide my hand,
    And struck, and struck, and heard the hell-hounds
    bark ;
And I fell beneath a horse, but I reached with all
    my force,
    And ripped him with my reap-hook through the
    dark.

As we struggled, knowing not whose hand was at
    our throat,
    Whose blood was spouting warm into our eyes,
We felt the thick snow-drift swoop upon us from
    the rift,
    And murmur in the pauses of our cries ;
But, lo ! before we wist, rose the black reek and
    the mist,
    And the pale Moon made a glamour from the skies.

O God! it was a sight that made the hair turn
  white,
  That withered up the heart's blood into woe,
To see the faces loom in the dimly lighted gloom,
  And the dead men lying bloodily below;
While melting, with no sound, fell with gentleness
  around
  The white peace and the wonder of the Snow!

Ay, and thicker, thicker, poured the pale silence of
  the Lord,
  From the hollow of His hand we saw it shed,
And it thickened round us there, till we choked
  and gasped for air,
  And beneath was ankle-deep and stainéd red;
And soon, whatever wight was smitten down in
  fight
  Was buried in the drift ere he was dead.

Then we beheld at length the troopers in their
  strength,
  For faster, faster, faster, up they streamed,
And their pistols flashing bright showed their faces
  ashen white,

And their blue steel caught the driving moon
and gleamed.
And a dying voice cried, 'Fly!' And behold, e'en
at the cry,
A panic fell upon us, and we screamed!

Oh, shrill and awful rose, 'mid the splashing blood
and blows,
Our scream unto the LORD that let us die;
And the Fiend amid us roared his defiance at the
LORD,
And his servants slew the strong man 'mid his
cry;
And the LORD kept still in heaven, and the only
answer given
Was the white Snow falling, falling, from the sky.

Then we fled! the darkness grew! 'mid the driving
cold we flew,
Each alone, yea, each for those whom he held
dear;
And I heard upon the wind the thud of hoofs behind,
And the scream of those who perished in their fear,

But I knew by heart each path through the darkness
of the strath,
And I hid myself at dawn,—and I am here.

Ah! gathered in one fold be the holy men and old,
And beside them lie the curséd and the proud;
The Howiesons are there, and the people of Glen Ayr,
Kirkpatrick, and Macdonald, and Macleod.
And while the widow groans, lo! God's hand around
their bones
His thin ice windeth softly as a shroud.

11

Ay, on mountain and in vale our women will look
    pale,
  And palest where the ocean surges boom;
Buried 'neath snow-drift white, with no holy prayer
    or rite,
  Lie the lovéd ones they look for in the gloom;
And deeper, deeper still, drops the Snow on vale
    and hill,
  And deeper and yet deeper is their Tomb!

THE NORTHERN MUSE.

BELL from the North hath journeyed hither;
    She brings the scent of heather with her,
To show in what sweet glens she grew.
Where'er she trips, in any weather,
She steps as if she trod on heather,
    And leaves a sense like dropping dew.

The mountains own her for their daughter;
Her presence feels like running water,
    Cooled from the sun in a green glade:
So strange she seems to city seeing,—
A playmate of the winds,—a being
    Made of the dew and mountain shade.

In the strange streets she stops to listen,
Her red lips part, her blue eyes glisten,
    Wild windy voices round her speak;

She sees the streets roll dark and clouded,
Fearless as when she paused, enshrouded
　　By mists upon a mountain-peak.

And oft, while wondrous-eyed she wanders,
She meets a sweet face,—pauses, ponders,—
　　And then peers backward as she goes;
As in the far-off solemn places
She drooped the tenderest of faces
　　Over some tender thing that grows.

Long have the clouds and winds been by her,
Long have the waters murmured nigh her,
　　And sweet delight in those hath she;
Long has she watched the shapes of wonder
Darken around with crying thunder,
　　Yet all have used her tenderlie.

Yea, she hath been a frail flower, lying
Under the peak where storms were crying,
　　Feeling the hills quake through and through,
And, when the storm was ended, raising
A little dewy head, and gazing
　　With pensive pleasure up the blue.

Yea, then the serpent lightning often
Watched her with eyes that seemed to soften,
And smiled, and fled, and smiled again;

Till, all around her gentler growing,
She felt the moist winds blowing, blowing,
   While shafts of cool light drank the rain.

When mighty shapes had love and pity,
What should appal her in the city?
   What should she fear in sun or shower?
The cloud of life is pleasure-laden,
She fears it not,—she is a maiden
   Familiar with the things of power.

She is as sweet as maidens may be,
Yet does not seem as things of clay be,
   But seemeth, as she passes by,
The shadow of a spirit-lady
(A wool-white cloud with image shady)
   Floating above her in the sky!

Yet seems she made in mortal fashion,—
A thing of pureness and of passion,
   A winning thing of eyes and lips,
A maiden with a cheek to sigh on,
A heart to love, a breast to die on,
   Kiss-worthy to the finger-tips!

No pantaloon, no simpering sinner,
No little man of straw shall win her,
  No scented darling of the sun;
But he who wins must win in honour,
And stir her soul, and breathe upon her,
  Even as the shapes of power have done.

And such a one his plaint should utter
Where the torn wings of tempests flutter,
  Where waters stir and winds are loud;
Or in the dark mysterious city,
When she is stirred to human pity,
  In the windy motion of the cloud.

Bell from the North, how shall I win her?
Wind, cloud, shade, water dwell within her,
  And she, like those, is meek and strong.
How shall I weave, O mountain daughter,
A song of wind, cloud, shade, and water?
  How make thee mine with such a song?

Lo! here the things of power are meaner,
The flowers around our feet uncleaner,
  Than where her vagrant footsteps climb;

And here we prize ignoble thinking,
And here sit latter rhymesters drinking
   The muddy lees of ancient rhyme.

And, oh! the singing must be mournful;
Strong things are cruel, sweet things scornful,
   And the fresh breath of life grows foul;
While where she roams strong things are tender,
Great things are grand things, sounds of splendour
   Drown the dull hooting of the owl.

The life-cloud round me thunders, lightens;
Strong without gentleness, it frightens
   The timid soul to grovelling deeds;
And when the brave soul, hating error,
Upbraids the many-headed terror,
   It smites him down, and no man heeds.

If, ere the song be uttered duly,
I who have served her long and truly
   Should faint and fall, though strong and brave,
Last I will pray in loving duty
That Bell will come, with all her beauty,
   To look a little on my grave.

And she will come (while up above her
The spirit-lady still will hover,
　　Pausing a space, with white wings furled);
Her foot will rest, her eye look nor'ward,
And that one grave will be thenceforward
　　The sweetest grave in all the world.

And surely, when she wanders thither,
The scent of heather will be with her,
　　The shady peace of mountains blue;
And she will breathe like fresh winds blowing,
And glide away like water flowing,
　　And leave a sense like dropping dew.

THE BALLAD-MAKER.

(LONDON.)

STOP! that's your training. You 're too hard, I say,
   Far, far too hard on those that go astray:
There's something to be said, by folk who feel,
For girls that step astray, and lads who steal,
And they are human souls in sin's despite.
'T is hard to find one's way without a light
Through this dark world, seeking the bit o' bread;
And being good comes after being fed.
If you had seen as much of town as me,
As much of wickedness and misery,
You'd look on townsfolk with a friendlier gaze;
But you are from the country, and their ways
Look black beside the life that you have led,

How did I know that you were country bred?
Ah, that's a trick I keep, though I am gray;

For once I lived in Sussex, far away;
And though full forty years have passed, and more,
I know a country face among a score,
By tokens that I catch before it flies—
Dress, voice, and something cow-like in the eyes.
Ay, and whene'er a coster girl I meet
Selling her violets up and down the street,
Or see a country cart go past with hay,
It seems I lived in Sussex yesterday,
And I can see the salt green marsh, and hear
The washing of the waters low and clear,
And see the silver sails out in the bay
Come in the moon like ghosts, and dip, and melt away.

Yes, friend, I am the man who makes the rhyme;
Much have I made and sold too in my time:
This room is papered with them, big and small,
So that a man can read them on the wall.
And they are but a few of those I made,
Since I began the task and found it paid.
There 's one that every 'prentice boy has read,—
How Tommie Thresher shot his sweetheart dead;
And that 's another on the poisoner Brown,
And there 's a comic song that took the town.

But these are poor weak things, although they pay;
There's something in me better far than they!
There's nothing in them fine, and fresh, and true,—
They jingle, but they never thrill one through,
Like some by other men that I have read.
But I should like for once, ere I am dead,
To write a thing more true, and fresh, and fair,
Fit for poor folk whose hearts are full of care.
Why, if a man, just by a rhyme, could show
How fresh the winds down in the country blow,
How by the sea the marsh smells salt and sweet,
Or how the bird cries 'cuckoo' in the heat,
Or if a man his feelings could write down
When flower girls sell their flowers about the town,
Or put in music all the frets and fears
Of townsfolk, the deep murmur in their ears,
The crying out for sleep, the fight for bread,
The strange hard thoughts they feel when they lay
    down their dead.

Ah, many a night I've tried to speak my mind,—
I wanted learning, though, as now I find;
The rhymes would never answer as they ought,
Or, coming, killed the feeling and the thought.

And so I found 'twas useless waste of time,
But turned again to money-making rhyme,
Where thoughts and feelings were of small ado,
So that the words were strong, the jingle true;
And when the printer sold 'em far and wide,
Was fool enough to feel a kind of pride.

Last year I tried it hard, but all in vain,
Although my heart was full of a sharp pain,
Because my little neighbour, up on high,
Was taken badly, and about to die,—
Little Jem Hart, half coster lad, half thief,
One of the sort you wish to bring to grief;
Only sixteen, and with his spine amiss,—
So thin, that when he raised his hand like this,
You saw the yellow sunlight shining through.

He had been bred among a wicked crew,
And ne'er a friend in all the world had he,—
Never a friend in all the world but me,
To nurse him, shake the straws to make his bed,
And stuff with rags a pillow for his head.
For hope was gone—he knew that he must die;
But life was dismal, and he did not cry,
And wore away with little pain—up there.

And so, whenever I had time to spare,
I sat by Jem, and tried to give him cheer;
And he was thankful from his heart, poor dear!
And proud he had at least one friend to stay
Beside him watching as he went away.
And though he said but little, now and then
He startled me with what he knew of men:
For it was terrible how one so young
Could have such crafty sayings on his tongue;
And sore to look on one so weak and wan,
A child, yet weary as an old, old man.

He knew full well his time was short below,
And yet his heart was not afraid to go;
And when I sunk my voice and took his hand,
And talked to him about a better land,
He seemed to think it sure no place could be
More dull than London was to such as he.
But now and then, when he could hear the cries
Of boys outside, a sharp look filled his eyes,
And his thin hand hung heavier on mine.

And it was summer, and the days were fine,
And through the smoky glass the light came red,

And tinted little Jem upon his bed;
And he would wake for hours, and watch the pane,
Until it dazzled him to sleep again.
And he would have strange dreams, and toss, and moan,
And cry to some one to be let alone,
Whining for fear; and often it would seem
He stole or picked a pocket in his dream,
And drew breath hard, hearing the folk rush by,
And ran till he was caught, and wakened with a cry.

It was a sight to make a man's heart ache
To sit like me up there and see him wake
From one of those hard dreams; for 'Dick,' he said,
'Give me your hand—I thought that I was dead.'
And then, afraid, he told me all he dreamed.
He thought he was in Heaven, and it seemed
Pleasant and bright and green like Primrose Hill,
And there was no one there, but all was still;
And he was clean and naked, and the light
Shone on his body, and made it golden bright;
And though a little hungry, through his breast
He felt a tired and pleasant peace and rest.
Then, seeing no one nigh, and tired, he crept
Into a corner full of flowers, and slept.

But all at once, while lying on the sod,
He heard a deep gruff voice, and knew 't was GOD,
And felt rough fingers seize him by the ears,
While he was thick with sleep, and full of fears;
And heard GOD say, 'What boy lies here apart?'
And some one said it was the thief, Jem Hart;
And though he sobbed and cried, they would not hark,
But took him to a gateway, cold and dark,
And thrust him out—and full of pain he woke.

Pale was his face and fearful as he spoke:
But when I answered him in cheerful style,
I coaxed his poor pinched features to a smile.
And lying back he watched the smoky pane,
And hearkened to the people down the lane,
In silence thinking till his eyelids closed;
But, looking up o' sudden as he dozed,
He pressed my hand more tight, and held his head,—
'Dick, say some bits of poetry,' he said.

I stared at first, because it seemed so new;
But, after pondering what to say and do,
I murmured low some things that I had made,—
Fine-sounding things, that took the town and paid;

13

And Jem closed eyes, and noted every one,
And kept as still as stone till I had done,
And hearkened to the rhyme as one might list
To the clock's ticking, careless though he missed
The meaning of the ditty, sad or glad.

But when my stock was done, and still the lad
Asked me to tell him more, I called to thought
A poor thing I had made when overwrought,
One of those weary times I tried in vain
To put in honest verse my own heart's pain ;
And I was troubled, as I said it o'er,
By feelings written down so long before,
And my voice broke,—my throat was full of tears,—
The sounding city murmured in my ears,—
I felt Jem's hand between my fingers creeping,
And, looking down, I saw that little Jem was weeping.

Then I was touched to see him grieving so,
And clasped his hand, and spoke more sad and low,
Peering upon his face ; and as I spoke,
Instead of the low hum of city folk,
I heard the washing sea upon the shore ;
And when I had said the silly verses o'er,

'Say it again!' cried little Jem; and when,
To please his heart, I said the song again,

In through the smoky glass the setting sun
Gleamed sickly, and the daý was nearly done.

I.

Oh, London is a dismal city,
    When one is all alone,
And it's hard to keep your heart up
    When your friends are dead and gone ;
And what is the good of living,
    And struggling bitterly, wet or dry ?
It's better just to shut your eyes,
    And lie down on your back and die!

II.

Oh, who would struggle and struggle
    To get the bit of bread,
Who would be cold and weary,
    With an aching heart and weary head,
When all in the dark still earth
    Quiet and peaceful you can lie ?
Then isn't it better to close your eyes,
    And lie down on your back and die ?

III.

There's green fields, flowers, and cresses
    In the place where I was born,
And you hear the waters of the sea
    A-sounding night and morn;
But London city is dismal work,
    And your heart feels lonely as the days go by;
Then isn't it better to close your eyes,
    And lie down on your back and die?

That was the song, and o'er and o'er to him
I murmured it until mine eyes were dim,
And my heart ached again;—for all the time
There seemed a kind of magic in the rhyme,
And I could hear the washing sea, and smell
The salt green marshes where I used to dwell,
And see the grim room melt around me, showing
The water trembling, and the fresh breeze blowing,
And white-sailed fish-boats dipping in the breeze.

But while my heart was full of things like these,
The evening came; and when the pale moonlight
Crept o'er the house-tops, dim and dusky bright,

The arm of little Jem grew heavy as lead,
And, looking down, I saw that he was dead.

And even then, far, far away, I seemed
Staring down dumbly at a face that gleamed
On water in the moonlight silver clear,
And though 't was night, full plainly I could hear
The bird that comes when summer days are blue,
Crying afar away, 'Cuckoo! cuckoo! cuckoo!'

Ah! many a time, amid the hum of town,
I 've tried my best to put such feelings down:
Full oft they come, they go; but when I try
To hold them fast, they turn to mist, and die.

THE BROOK.

OH, sweet and still around the hill
    Thy silver waters, Brook, are creeping;

Beneath the hill as sweet and still
  Thy weary friend lies sleeping:
A laurel leaf is in his hair,
  His eyes are closed to human seeming,
And surely he has dreams most fair,
  If he indeed be dreaming.

O Brook, he smiled, a happy child,
  Upon thy banks, and loved thy crying,
And, as time flew, thy murmur grew
  A trouble purifying;
Till, last, thy laurel leaf he took,
  Dream-eyed and tearful, like a woman,
And turned thy haunting cry, O Brook,
  To speech divine and human.

O Brook! in song full sweet and strong
  He sang of thee he loved so dearly;
Then softly creep around his sleep,
  And murmur to him cheerly;
For though he knows nor fret nor fear,
  Though life no more slips strangely through him,
Yet he may sleep more sound to hear
  His friend so close unto him.

And when at last the sleepers cast
   Their swathes aside, and, wondering, waken,
Let thy friend be full tenderlie
   In silver arms uptaken.
Him be it then thy task to bear
   Up to the Footstool, softly flowing,—
Smiles on his eyes, and in his hair
   Thy leaf of laurel blowing!

14

THE NORTHERN WOOING.

(NORTH COAST.)

S KIES are dusky, winds are keen,
Round Lallan Farm on Hallowe'en.

All is dark across the night,
But, see! one crimson glare of light.

What are those that in the air
Flit against the crimson glare?

Falling flakes of snow they seem,
Or night-moths gathered by the gleam.

Round and round they wind and wind.—
Tiny shades against the blind.

Child, wish now! while thou canst see!
'T is the faëry companie!

O'er thy shoulder peep; and so
Behold thy future bedfellów.

Once a year, on Hallowe'en,
Are the faëry people seen.

Thus round happy farms they fly,
While the peat-fire blazes high.

Lad and lass, to-night beware!
There is magic in the air!

*   *

'Ah, bairns, my bairns, forbear on Hallow Night
To mock the folk o' faëry and their might,
For though ye deem these things are all untrue,
Yourselves may be the first to see and rue!
Hark! now the wind a moment sinks and dies,
Hear ye not low faint voices and strange cries
Outside the door, and flutterings on the pane

Of little finger-taps, like gentle rain?
Ay! 't is the folk o' faëry hovering nigh :
Draw back the blind to peep, and they will fly ;
But serve them maidenly, with charm and spell,
And the old customs that they love so well,
And they will show you all you wish to see,—
Your true-love's face, his country and degree,—
All, all a lass with pleasure asks and learns,
Down to the very number of her bairns.

'Aye please the fays ! 't is easy if ye will ;
But woe be yours if they should wish ye ill :
Your joe will take to drink, or drown at sea,
Or find another sweeter companie ;
Your cheeks will droop, your een will lose their light ;
Ye 'll marry an old man, and freeze at night !
In vain, in vain ye seek to change your fate,
When they have fixed your lot and future mate ;
In vain ye seek to frown and turn aside,—
They make your heart consent in spite of pride.
'T was so with me, when I was young and gay,
Though I was loth to hearken and obey.
They led me to their choice by spells and charms ;
They closed my eyes, and drew me to his arms !

Or grandfather had ne'er prevailed on me
To droop my pride, and smile as low as he.

'For, though I say it, bairns, my face was fair,
And I was Farmer Binnie's child and heir;
A widowed father's pet, I ruled the place,
Right proud, be sure, of fortune and of face.
My hair was golden then, like Maggie's here,
And I had een as sly, yet crystal clear,
And I could look as bright when pleased and fain,
Or toss my curls with just as sweet disdain!
What wonder, then, if half the country-side
Looked bairns into my face, and blushed and cried,
Bleating behind me, like a flock of sheep
Behind a shepherd-lass, who, half asleep,
Counts them in play, leads them with pretty speech,
Rates all alike, and scarce knows each from each?
One found me coy, another found me gleg,
Another skittish as the gray mare Meg;
Just as the humour took me, I was wild
Or gentle,—one day cross, the next day mild;
But cared no more for handsome Jamie West,
When he came o'er the heather in his best,
Jingling his silver spurs at our fire-end,
In breeks so tight 'twas near his death to bend,
Than for the grim old Laird of Glumlie Glen,
Who rode on solemn sheltie now and then

Over the moors,—and, making mouths at me,
With father cracked of crops o'er barley-bree,—
While Jock the groom, who knew I loved such fun,
Gingered the sheltie for a homeward run!

'Yet oft I tried to picture in my brain
What kind of laddie in the end would gain,
And vainly sought 'mong those around to find
The substance of the shadow in my mind.
But, bairns, in vain I pictured; and anew
Will you and children's children picture too :—
The bonnie shadow flies, and in its place
The chilly substance steals to our embrace.
I swore he should be stately, dark, and tall,—
His hair was fiery red and he was small;
I swore he should be rich in gold and lands,—
His fortune was the strength of his two hands;
I swore he should be meek and ruled by me,—
The De'il himself were easier led than he!'

*   ☉

Round the happy farm they flee,—
Faëry folk in companie.

Near the peat-blaze range in ring;
Fiddler, twang the fiddle-string.

In the great tub duck the head
After apples rosy red!

Slyly let each pair by turn
Watch the magic chestnuts burn!

Love who never loved before,—
Kiss me quick behind the door!

Lad and lass, to-night beware!
There is magic in the air!

*   *

'O bairns, we gathered round the blazing peat,
And lad and lass sat close and whispered sweet,
While ancient women spake of wonders seen
On many a long-forgotten Hallowe'en,
And old men nodded snowy polls the while,
Passing the snuff-box round with sceptic smile.
Tall in the midst my father had his place,
Health and a golden harvest in his face;

And, hand in his, full rosy and full sly,
Surrounded by my silly sheep, sat I.
Loud rang the laughter! fearless grew the fun!
Happy and warm at heart was every one!
The old, old shepherd, worn with rain and wind,
Blinked in the ingle-nook with eyes half blind,
While at his feet his tired old dog slept deep,
And, barking, dreamed of gathering the sheep.

' James West was there, the Laird, and many more,
Wooers both old and young, and rich and poor;
And, though I say it, bairns, that night I smiled
My sweetest, and their hearts were fairly wild.
Braw with new ribbons in my hair lint-light,
Clean as a guinea, newly minted, bright,
I sat and hearkened to their silly speech,
Happy, and with a careless smile for each;
And yet, though some were fine and fair to see,
Not one had power to steal my heart from me.

' Oh, Hallowe'en in those old times, I vow,
Was thrice as merry, thrice as sweet, as now!
The benches drawn aside, the supper o'er,
Fresh sand was strewn upon this very floor;

16

The fiddle played—the fiddler gave a squeal—
Up stood the folk, and father led the reel;
The lads louped up and kicked the beam for fun,
The crimson lassies screamed to see it done;
Meantime the old men, with contented look,
Smoked clean new cutties in the chimney nook,
And thought of days when they were young and gay,
And pleased the lassies, too, with feats of play.
Yet one there was, my bairns, amid the throng,
Who, though his years were young, his limbs full strong,
Danced not that night; but pale and gloomy, stayed
Among the gaffers, in the chimney shade,—
Hugh Scott his name, an orphan lad, whose hand
Guided the ploughshare on my father's land,
But one my father prized and trusted best
For cunning and for skill o'er all the rest.
Full well I knew the rogue esteemed me sweet,
But I was gentry, and his masters' meat,
And often smiled on him full fond and free,
As ne'er I smiled on those who courted me,
Pleased that my smiles sank sweet to his heart's core,
But certain he would never hope for more.

'There in the chimney shadow, pale and sad,

Clad in his clothes o' Sabbath, sat the lad :
In vain, to catch his look, the lassies leered,
In vain the old folk saw his sulks, and sneered,
But aye his dim and melancholy e'e
Turned glittering in the shade and followed me ;
Whene'er I danced with some fine wooer there,
I saw his fist clench and his eyeballs glare,—
Red as a rick on fire I saw him grow
Whene'er my partner whispered sweet and low,
And had a kiss been stolen in his sight,
I swear he would have ta'en revenge in fight.
Half pleased, half careless, to increase his ill,
I marked him kindly, as a lassie will,
And sent him many a smile of tender light
To cheer him in his nook, that Hallow Night.

' Louder the fiddler, warmed with many a glass,
Shouted to stir the hearts of lad and lass !
Faster and faster on his strings he skirled !
Faster and faster round the dancers whirled !
Close by, the young folks ducked for apples red,
Splashing, with puffing cheek and dripping head,
Into the washing-bine, or, in a ring,
With gaping mouths, they played at cherry-string.

But in the parlour, from the turmoil free,
My father sat with antique companie—
Cronies who mixed their tumblers strong and deep
Twelve times, and toddled sober off to sleep.

' But, bairns, 't was near the hour when ghaists are
        said
To rise white-sheeted from their kirkyard bed,
When the owl calls, and blinks his e'eball white,
In ruins, where the fairies flit by night.
And now my heart beat fast and thick for fear,
Because the time of spells and charms was near,
And I was bent that night alone to fly
Out o'er the meadow to the kiln,—and try
The twining charm, the spell of fairy fate,
And hear the name of him that I should mate.'

*   *

Lad and lass, to-night beware '
There is magic in the air!

Winds are crying shrill, and, hark !
Ghosts are groaning in the dark.

Who will dare this Hallow Night
Leave the happy ingle-light?

Who will dare to stand alone,
While the fairy thread is thrown?

Who this night is free from fear?
Let her ask,—and she shall hear!

*   *

'Dark, dark was all, as shivering and alone
I set my foot upon the threshold-stone,
And, trembling close, with twitching fingers caught
The great horn lanthorn from the stables brought,
And leant against the door to keep it wide,
And peered into the dreadful gloom, and sighed.
Black was the lift, and faintly fell the rain,
The wind was screeching like a ghaist in pain;
And, while I paused, and pinched my e'en to mark,
The wind swung to the door, and left me in the dark.

'O bairns! what would my foolish heart have gi'en
To let the fairies be that Hallowe'en!
But I had sworn, and all the lassies knew,

And I was shamed, and fain must see it through.
Oh, where were all my boasts, my laughter light,
Now I was there alone amid the night?
While faint far ben the farm the fiddle cried,
And far away the sound of dancing died.

'Thud, thud against my breast my wild heart leapt,
As out across the misty yard I crept,
Holding the lanthorn up, whose flickering ray
Made darkness doubly deep along the way.
Then in my ears I seemed to hear strange screams,
And awesome faces flashed with lightning-gleams,
And, as I wandered, fingers sharp and wee ·
Pinched me and pulled my garter o'er the knee,
And nipt my breasts (ay, laugh! your time is near!)
Yet still I held along, though sick with fear;
Out of the yard, across the field, the dew
Still drizzling blindly in my face, I flew,
Till, breathless, panting hard against the wind,
Fearful to look before me or behind,
I reached the kiln,—and, standing dizzy there,
Heard softer voices round me in the air,
A sound like little feet along the gloom,
And hummings faint, as of a fairy loom.

'Then setting down the lanthorn on the ground,
I entered in, nor paused to look around,

But faint and fast began to say the charm
All northern lasses know, and reached my arm,
Casting the twine, and holding one end tight—
Flinging the other loose into the night.
O bairns! O bairns! scarce had I uttered thrice
The fairy spell, with lips as cold as ice,
When through my blood a fearful shudder spread,
For ghaistly fingers tightened at the thread!
Then in a hollow voice, to know my doom,
"Who holds, who holds?" I cried, into the gloom,
And ere the echo of my voice had died,
"Hugh Scott! Hugh Scott!" a hollow voice replied;
And, screaming out, and covering up my face,
Kicking the lanthorn o'er, I fled the place,
Stumbling and tripping, flew across the field,
Till, white as any ghaist, I reached the bield,
And crept up to my room, and hid my head,
Moaning, among the blankets of the bed!'

                    *   *

            Lightly soon shall rise the sun!
            Fays, begone! your work is done.

            Fiddler, put your tools away,
            Take a nap among the hay.

Lads and lassies, flushed and red,
Yawn no more, but off to bed.

Maiden, thou hast heard and seen
Wonders strange at Hallowe'en.

Thou hast wished to hear and see—
And thy fate is fixed for thee.

Sad or merry, ill or well,
Fairy looms have spun the spell.

In among the blankets creep—
Dream about him in your sleep.

Wake and smile with heart resigned!
Kiss and cuddle, and be kind!

      *   *

'Oh, bitter was my heart, my wits amazed;
Wildly I pondered like a lassie crazed:
Hugh Scott my mate! Hugh Scott, of all around!
A pauper lad, a tiller of the ground!
When wealthy men came lilting o'er the lea,
In shining braws, and sought to marry me!

16

'Nay, nay!' I cried, and frowning raised my face,
'No force shall make me choose a lot so base:
The spirits of the air but wish this night
To try my heart, and fill my soul with fright;
Yet they shall know full soon they rate me ill,—
I fear them not, nor shall I work their will!'
But as I spoke, I shook, and unaware
Keeked o'er my shoulder at the glass, and there
In the faint lamplight burning by the bed,
His face, a moment mirror'd, came and fled!

'O bairns!—what further tale have I to tell?
How could I fight against a fate so fell?
Strive as I might, awaking or asleep,
I found my eyes in fascination deep
Follow Hugh Scott, and, till my heart went wild,
He haunted me from place to place, and smiled.
Then, unaware, to notice I began
That he was trim and stout, and like a man,
That there was winning sweetness in his tongue,
And that his voice was honeyed when he sung.
Nay, more, full soon his manners seemed to me
More fine than those of loftier degree,
And as for gold, though he was humble, still

He had a fortune in his farming skill.
Ay, bairns! before another Hallow Night
The fairies to their wish had worked me quite;
And, since his heart had ever favoured Hugh,
Full easily they won my father too—
And when at last Hugh craved me to be his,
I fell upon his heart and cried for bliss.

'Ah! heed not, bairns, though grandfather should swear
That, when I tried the spell, himsel' was there;
That, when I saw the phantom in the room,
He too, was near me, keeking through the gloom;
And that his craft and cunning were the charms
Which cheated me and drew me to his arms.
Nay! nay! but maidenly, with song and spell,
And the old customs that they love so well,
Serve ye the fays this night—be meek! be brave!
And though they may not give you all ye crave,
Be sure that you will find, as I have found,
Their choice right wise, and all their counsels sound,
And bless for many a year the love and light
They spin for happy hearts, on Hallow Night.

THE BALLAD OF THE STORK.

(SCANDINAVIA.)

THE widow on the storm-tost shore of Denmark
    had her home,
Under the shade of pleasant woods, close to the salt sea-
    foam ;
But little peace was in the hut, and grief was at the
    door,
For day and night the widow's thoughts were tossing
    far from shore.

To Him whose white foot stills the waves and bids the
    storm be done,
The widow prayed upon her knees, to send her back
    her son;
For God had sent a watery wind to blow the boy
    away,
And to the Indies he had sailed all on a summer's day.

' See, mother, mother !' cried the lad, 'thou hast not land
    nor gold ;
The dun cow, fastened to its ring, grows dry and waxes
    old,—
But, running silver from this cup, the water says to me,
"What fool would starve ashore when wealth is on the
    shining sea ?"'

And sticking in his cap a sprig of green, he kissed her lips,
And sprang away that summer day, and rowed among
    the ships ;
And, weeping, on the beach she stands,—sails fill and
    pennons fly,—
He stands on deck, and waves his cap—and the great
    ship goes by.

Three years she waited wearily, and watched with weary
    eyne,
And spun upon the threshold as she searched the straight
    sea-line ;
And pale she tossed on bed o' straw, and heard the
    waters moan,
And day still came and went at sea, and still she was
    alone.

Ah, little one! ah, wilful one! now are ye fast asleep!
The waters roar around your bones under the dreadful
    deep :
Your sleep is in the dark cold depths,—you cannot turn
    nor cry ;
No mother now may keep you warm, or kiss you where
    ye lie.'

To kirk she hied full wearily upon each holy day,
Yet little peace the kirk could give—she had no heart
    to pray ;
But in September, when they read the tale of other
    years,
About the widow's son of Nain, her heart was full to
    tears.

Then to the hut she weeping turned, and wearied on
    once more,
And sadly watched the tall ash tree that grew beside
    her door ;
For there a Stork had made his home for many a year,
    and he
Was now an ancient Stork, and knew full many a far
    countree.

For every autumn on the roof he stood and waved his
wing,
Then cloudwards rose, and in the wind went southward
travelling ;
And every spring on stately wing back to the hut he hied,
Far as the Red Sea had he fared, with summer for his
guide.

And now the widow saw him rise, less fleet of wing
and strong,
For now he was an ancient Stork, nor would his years
be long.
' Ah me !' she thought ; ' with thee, old friend, my laddie
played full sweet—
Green leaves he tied around thy neck, and gave thee
food to eat.

' Perchance thy sharp round eye hath seen what still is
hid from me—
My little one afloat and dead upon a glassy sea.
Here hast thou dwelt for many a year, and we have
watched thy nest,
But thou art powerless in thy turn to help my heart
to rest.'

How! powerless? God's mild will to work what thing
  is quite unmeet?
Where is the widow's wandered son? wrapt in his wind-
  ing-sheet?
Nay, on Morocco's blazing shore with slaves behold him
  stand,—
Weeping, he shakes a chain, and looks towards his
  native land.

He heeds not yonder sweet-eyed slave, who smiles to
  soothe his pain,
Nor yonder fat and·turbaned Turk, who holds him in
  his chain;
He thinks upon his mother's hut, he bites his bitter lips,
He strains his eyes, and in a mist of tears he sees the
  ships.

But suddenly he stares amazed, for near him on the sand,
With long spare legs and ancient air, he sees a stranger
  stand—
A Stork, a grim and ancient Stork, full dim and dull
  of e'e,
The picture of the Stork he knew within his own coun-
  tree.

' Ah! could it be indeed my old brave comrade travelling?
He hath the same bright beak and feet, the same black
   ruffled wing;

17

I seem to know the very walk, the solemn stately pace,
And I could almost swear he hath some memory of my
    face.'

'T is spring again in Denmark, and all is green once
    more,
' Spring comes again! the stork has come!' they cry
    upon the shore;
And all the folk wear feast-day dress, and the good
    priest is there;
And with the rest the widow stands, and looks into
    the air.

It is the Stork, the ancient Stork,—he lights upon the
    ground :
' Oh, see!' they cry, ' around his feet a paper tightly
    bound.'
They loose it then with eager hands, they open it and
    read,—
The widow screams, for here is wrought a miracle in-
    deed !

' O mother, here I dwell alive, but held in slaverie,
So gather, gather gold, and send a ransom o'er the sea.

If this should reach thy hands, bless GOD, who sent the
    bird to me.'—
And all the rest was guidance how to send and set him
    free.

Oh, who that Sabbath was so pinched as grudge from
    out his store
A silver mite to fill the plate they placed at the kirk
    door,
The cow-girl brought the piece of gold that was to
    buy a gown,
The beggar slyly neared the plate, and threw his beg-
    gings down.

Now in his mother's hut again the sailor sits once more,
Content to cast a fisher's net, nor wander far from shore,
But blessings on the ancient Stork, and honours three
    times three,
Who followed summer round the world, and set the
    sailor free !

SIGURD OF SAXONY.

(MEDIÆVAL.)

THE sedgy shores of this enchanted lake
  Are dark with shadows of the swans which make
    Their nests along its marge;
And on the hither side, where silver waves
Curl with low music into hollow caves,
    Waiting for that bright barge
Which beareth sleepers to the silent land,
I, Sigurd, in my ghostly sorrow, stand.

I stand alone beneath heaven's silent arch,
Shaded both night and day by clouds that march
    And countermarch above;
A sombre suit of perfect mail I wear,
A gloomy plume, that troubles the thin air
    To murmurs if I move;
My sword is red and broken; and my shield
Bears a gold anchor on a sable field.

This is a place where mortals find not speech ;
Save the small murmurous waves that crawl the beach,

All is as still as death:
I hear my heart against my ribs of stone,
Like to a wild bird in the net, make moan;
 My slow and frozen breath
Curls like a vapour o'er the silent spot;
My shadow seeks my feet, and moveth not.

Nought can redeem her. Wherefore I seek grace
To join her in her distant dwelling-place
 Of pastoral repose;
And I would make this heart that aches and grieves
As white and perfect as a lily's leaves
 And fragrant as a rose,
That with a stainless spirit I may take
The solemn barge across the enchanted lake.

For, having worn her stainless badge in fight,
Thrice conquering in her name, by day and night
 I rode with vizor down,
Meeting and slaying honourable foes,
Wounded in flesh, giving and taking blows,
 To compass her renown.
Thus, warring a sweet war without reprieve,
I, Sigurd, wore her badge upon my sleeve.

Arméd from head to heel, with spear in hand,
I cried her praises through the wondering land,
    And few her praise refused;
Then flushing with my victory complete,
I hastened back and knelt me at her feet,
    Battered, and maimed, and bruised;
And then I wooed her in a secret place,
With light upon me from her shining face.

She bathed my bloody brow, with red wounds striped,
And with a kerchief white as snow she wiped
    The foam from off my mouth;
She set my unhelmed head upon her knee,
And wound white arms about me tenderly,
    And slaked the thirsty drouth
That ebbed in sluggish fire through blood and
    brain,
From a full cup of cool white porcelain.

Wherefore my soul again was strong. I caught
The voiceless music of her form and thought.
    I knelt upon my knee,
Saying, 'I love thee more than life or fame;
I love thee only less than my good name,

'Which is a part of thee;
And I adore thy beauty undefiled !'
Whereat she looked into mine eyes and smiled.

I wooed her night and day with virtuous deeds,
And that humility which intercedes
          With ladies for true men.
I took her lily of a hand in mine,
Drinking her breath, as soft as eglantine,
          And wooing well; and then
She toyed with my great beard, and gave consent:
So down the flowery path of love we went.

Twined closely, down the soft descent of love
We wandered on, with golden stars above,
          And many flowers below,
Until we came to this dark lake or sea,
Which openeth upon eternity,
          And could no farther go;
For beyond life and death, and these dark skies,
The place of sleep, the Silent Valley, lies.

Here on the beach we stood, and hand in hand
Waited to wander to that silent land,

And all the shore was dark;
Saying, ' We yearn to see the Happy Vale,
And hand in hand together we will sail

18

In the enchanted barque.'
Too late to turn: one passage we must take
Across the gleaming silence of the lake.

She said, 'The waters make such threatening moan,
Neither can pass across their waste alone;
        We cannot, cannot part;
We will together cross these waves of death.'
But the dark waves grew darker, and the breath
        Came colder from the heart;
And by each face a quiet cloud was worn,
Small as the shadow of a lamb new born.

Then in the distant waves we could behold
A radiance like the blowing autumn gold
        Of woodland forests deep;
And my sweet lady trembled, growing white
As foam of ocean on a summer night,
        When the wild surges leap;
And falling very cold upon my breast,
She faltered, 'I am weary,—let me rest.'

I laid her down upon a flowery bed,
And put soft mosses underneath her head,

And kissed her, and she slept;
And the air brightened round her, as the far
Blue ether burns like silver round a star.
 And round her slumber crept
A trouble of the air, and silver clear
The ghostly light upon the lake grew near.

Yea, nearer, nearer grew the light, and soon,
Shaped like the sickle of the early moon,
 The barge drew shoreward slow—
A vapour and a radiance all around,
A gleaming of fair faces, and a sound
 Of flutes and lute-strings low.
And round my lady crept a shadowy crowd,
Fading and brightening like a moonlit cloud.

They clustered with a ghostly light around
My lady dear, and raised her from the ground,
 And bare her to the barque;
Whereon I would have followed, but a hand
Held me like iron to the hated land.
 Then all again was dark;
And from the breathing darkness came a hum
Of voices sweet, 'Thy time has not yet come.'

And then I shrieked in utter agony;
While fading far away upon the sea
        I saw the light again;
And with a cry into the waves I sprung,
And sought to follow, but the waters clung
        About me like a chain;
And thrice I fought amid their rage and roar,
And thrice they hurled me bleeding on the shore.

Long have I waited here, alone, alone,
Hearing the melancholy waves make moan
        Upon the pebbly beach:
With eyes upon the pitiless stars above
Here have I waited in my homeless love,
        Pale, patient, deaf to speech,
With the salt rheum upon me, pale and bent,
And breathless as a marble monument.

This lonely watching would invite despair
Did I not oft catch glimpses of my fair
        Lady, so sadly lost,
Making, with radiance round her like a star,
A luminous pathway on the hill afar,
        Then fading like a ghost;

What time I shout aloud, and at the shout
Pause, shuddering at the echoes round about.

Twice has the barge returned: once for a bent
Old servitor, who, down the soft descent
        That leads to this dim land,
Had wandered from the towns that lie behind,
And, groping in the cold, had fall'n stone-blind
        Upon the shifting sand;
Once for a little gold-haired child astray,
Who, wandering hither, fell to sleep at play.

Twice has the mystic barge returned, and twice
Have I been frozen to the earth in ice,
        Helpless to move or speak;
Thrice have I fought with the relentless roar
Of water, and been flung upon the shore
        Battered, and maimed, and weak;
But now I wait with quiet heart and brain,
Grown patient with unutterable pain.

And I *will* wait. To slay myself were sin,
And I, self-slaughtered, could not hope to win
        My solitary boon;

But if the barge should come again, and leave
Me still in lonely watch without reprieve,
    Under the silver moon
I will lie down upon my back and rest,
With mailéd hands crossed praying on my breast;

And fall to slumber on a bed of weeds,
A knight well worn in honourable deeds,
    Yet lost to life, and old;
And haply I may dream before I wake
That I am floating o'er the pathless lake
    In that bright barge of gold;
And, waking, I may see with sweet surprise
Light shining on me from my lady's eyes.

A POEM TO DAVID.*

I.

I WOULD not be lying yonder,
   Where thou, belovéd, art lying,
Though the nations should crown me living,
   And murmur my praises dying.

Better this fierce pulsation,
   Better this aching brain,
Than dream, and hear faintly above me
   The cry of the wind and the rain;

Than lie in the kirkyard lonely,
   With fingers and toes upcurled,
And be conscious of never a motion
   Save the slow rolling round of the world.

* David Gray, Author of "The Luggie, and other Poems."

I would not be lying yonder,
  Though the seeds I had sown were springing !
I would not be sleeping yonder,
  And be done with striving and singing !

For the eyes are blinded with mildew,
  The lips are clammy with clay,
And worms in the ears are crawling,—
  But the brain is the brain for aye !

The brain is warm and glowing,
  Whatever the body be ;
It stirs like a thing that breatheth,
  And dreams of the Past and To be !

Ay ! down in the deep damp darkness
  The brains of the dead are hovelled !
They gleam on each other with radiance,
  Transcending the eye that is shrivelled '

Each like a faint lamp lighteth
  The skull wherein it dwelleth !
Each like a lamp turneth brighter
  Whenever the kirk-bell knelleth '

I would not be lying yonder
  Afar from the music of things,
Not were my green grave watered
  By the tears of queens and kings.

If the brain like a thing that breatheth
  Is full of the Past and To be,
The silence is far more awful
  Than the shriek and the agony;

And the hope that sweetened living
  Is gone with the light of the sun,
And the struggle seems wholly over,
  And nothing at all seems done;

And the dreams are heavy with losses,
  And sins, and errors, and wrongs,
And you cannot hear in the darkness
  If the people are singing your songs!

There's only the slow still rolling
  Of the dark world round and round,
Making the dream more wondrous,
  Though it render the sleep more sound.

'T is cold, cold, cold and weary,
　Cold in a weary place:
The sense of the sin is present
　Like the gleam of a demon's face!

What matter the tingling fingers
　That touch the song above you?
What matter the young man's weeping,
　And longing to know you and love you?

Nought has been said and uttered,
　Nought has been seen or known,—
Detraction, the adder above you,
　Is sunned on the cold grave-stone.

II.

Yet 't is dark here, dark,
　And the voices call from below!
'T is so dark, dark, dark,
　That it seems not hard to go'

'T is dark, dark, dark,
  And we close our eyes and are weary !
'T is dark, dark, dark,
  And the waiting seems bitter and dreary !

And yonder the sun is shining,
  And the green, long grass hath grown,
And the cool kirk-shade looks pleasant,
  And you lie so alone, so alone !

The world is heartless and hollow,
  And singing is sad without you,
And I think I could bear the dreaming
  Were mine arms around about you ;

Were thy lips to mine, belovéd,
  And thine arms around me too,
I think I could lie in silence,
  And dream as we used to do !

The flesh and the bones might wither,
  The blood be dried like dew,
The heart might crumble to ashes,
  Till dust was dust anew ;

And the world with its slow still motion
Might roll on its heavenward way,—
And our brains upon one another
Would gleam till the Judgment Day!

A SCOTTISH ECLOGUE.*

(NORTH COAST.)

SANDIE.

O LORD above, Thy wrath is swift and deep!
And yet by grace Thou sanctionest Thy sheep;
And blest are they who till the day o' doom,
Like haddocks, bear the marking of Thy thumb;
And curst, in spite of works and prayers, are they
On whom Thy mark has ne'er been printed sae.
For while the non-elected lie beneath,
And fast in flaming fire, and gnash their teeth,
Above their heads, where streams of honey spring,
Thy Elders stand in shining sarks, and sing,
And bless Thy Name for present gifts and past. .
O wife, John Galloway is gone at last!

* See *ante*, p. 63, AN ENGLISH ECLOGUE.

JEANIE.

Dead? Weel, we are all bound to GOD's abode,
And John has started first upon the road.
A Christian man and kind was John, indeed,
And free o' siller unto folk in need:
Ay, many a house will want now he is cold!
But GOD will give him back his gifts tenfold.

SANDIE.

O Jeanie Gourlay! keep thy clapper still;
It talks o' things you understand but ill:
I doubt, I sorely doubt, John Galloway
Is 'neath the oxter* o' the De'il this day:
True, in the way o' sinful flesh, his mind
Was charitable, and his heart was kind;
But light he lacked as long as he drew breath,
And lost the Eldership before his death;
And he had many a ghostly whispering
To tell he was a miserable thing,
Doomed by the wisdom of the Just to be
Condemned with those who graceless live and dee.

* Armpit.

Ay, grace, I fear, John Galloway was denied,
Though loud and oft for grace he groaned and cried.

'Sandie,' he used to say, 'I fear, I fear
I have no right among the holy here ;
I fear, I fear that I am in the dark—
The LORD on me forgot to put His mark.
I canna steel my heart to folk who sin,
I canna put my thoughts to discipline ;
Oft when I pray, I hear Him whisper plain,
"Jock Galloway, pray awa', but 't is in vain ; "—
Nae sweet assurance arms me 'gainst the De'il,
Nae happy faith, like that my fellows feel :
I long for GOD, I beg Him on my knee,
But fear He hath to wrath previsioned me !'

JEANIE.

Poor man ! his strife was sore ; but, Sandie, mind,
Nae man can tell what folks are predestined ;
Ev'n Sandie Gourlay may be one the De'il
Hath liberty to catch within his creel !

SANDIE.

Oh, blasphemy ! Thou fool, forbear and cease !
The sign o' grace is perfect faith and peace,
Such as the LORD, in spite o' many a cross,
Vouchsafes to men like me and neighbour Ross.

But Galloway ever was a braxie sheep,
A whining thing who dug his doubts too deep.
Why, mind ye, when old Robin Caird himsel'—
A heretic, a rogue, a man o' Bel,
Averring written Scripture was a lee,
And GOD was hard, stretched out his limbs to dee,
John by the sinner knelt and offered prayers:
'LORD GOD,' he said, 'pity his poor white hairs!
Be kind unto him! Take him unto Thee!'
And paid the coffin and the burial fee.
'Sandie,' he said, when Caird was in his grave,
'I doubt I am less holy than the lave:*
My blood is milk, and I am weak o' brain,—
O LORD, it broke my heart to see his pain!
I thought—I dared to think—if I were GOD,
Poor Caird should never gang so dark a road,
And thought—ay, dared to think, the LORD forgi'e!—
To think the LORD was crueller than me;
Forgetting GOD is just, and knoweth best
What folk should burn in fire, what folk be blest.'
Such was his nature, neither strong nor deep,—
Unlike the stern strong leaders of His sheep:

* The rest.

20

We made an Elder of John Galloway!
Large seemed his heart, he ne'er was known to stray;
But he had little strength or wrath severe—
He softened at the sinful pauper's tear;
He gript his purse and pleaded like a fool
For every lassie on the cuttie-stool.

JEANIE.

Where had the parish bairns sae kind a friend?

SANDIE.

Bairns? did he teach them grace, and make them mend?
At Sunday School what lad or lass had care
For fear o' flaming Hell, if John was there,—
Questioning blushing brats upon his knees,
And slyly slipping in their hands bawbees? *
Once while he talked to me o' life and death,
I smelt the smell o' whisky in his breath.
'Drinking again, John Galloway?' I said;
As gray as this pipe-reek, he hung his head.
'O Sandie, Sandie!' he replied, 'I ken
I am indeed the weakest man o' men.

* Halfpence.

Strange doubts torment me daily, and, alas!
I try to drown them in the poisoned glass.
By fits I fear! and in my chamber say,
LORD, *is* Thy mark on poor John Galloway?
And sorely troubled, stealing slyly out,
I try in drink to drown the imp o' Doubt.'
Woman, is this the man ye would defend?
Nay, wheesht awhile, and hearken to his end.
When he fell sick, in Martinmas, his fears;
Grew deeper far; I found him oft in tears;
Though from the prophets of GOD's might I read,
He hearkened, but was little comforted,
And even 'Revelations' had no power
To soothe the pangs of his departing hour.
A week before he left this vale of woe,
He at his window sat, and watched the snow
Falling and falling down without a sound,
Poured slowly from GOD's hand upon the ground:
'See, Sandie, how it snaws!' I heard him say;
'How many folk are cold, cold, cold this day!
How many want the fire that's warming me!
How many starve!—and yet why should it be?'
And when I took the Book, explained, and read,
He only gave a groan and shook his head.

'Clearer and clearer I perceive my sin,
How I to grace may never enter in;
That Book is for the strong, but I am weak.'—
And trembled, and a tear was on his cheek.

JEANIE.

Poor man! poor man! small peace on earth he found.

SANDIE.

The day he died, he called the elders round,
Shook hands, and said, 'Friends, though I gang from
        here,
Down under earth, all will at last be clear.
Too long have I been dwelling in the dark,
The LORD on me forgot to put His mark,
GOD help me!' And, till he was cold as clay,
His foolish lips had little more to say;
Yet after we had laid him down in dust,
Weak to the last we found him, and unjust;
For when his will was read, unto our shame,
The kirk was scarcely mentioned in the same!
But he had left what little gold he had
To Caird's sick widow and her lass and lad!

THE SAINT'S STORY.

(FRANCE, 13—.)

LA BELLE DAME Sans Mercy
Seldom knelt on her knee
To Saints of any degree
Ere she made a Saint of me!

Listen now as spirits can,
Spirit of the sacristan,
    And come and join me where I smile,
Sitting cross-legged on my own
Effigy, cut out in stone!
    Let us chatter for a while!

How quietly, amid the moonshine faint,
The full-length figure of the blessed Saint
(Myself), with wrinkled brow and broken nose,
Eyes closed and full of dust, upturnéd toes,

And hands so meekly folded on his breast,
Lies in the melancholy crypt at rest;
See! how the round eye of the moon looks through
  'The shapes embroidered on the window-panes,
Saints and Madonnas—purple, orange, blue—
  And with their ghosts the marble pavement stains;
Mark, too, the faint religious mist,
      Azure and amethyst!
Wherein along the fretted aisle and dim
The shadows of the good stalk now and hymn
      The distant cherubim!
Come, sit cross-legged and talk,
And watch them as they walk!
You with your pinched and melancholy face,
Your little nose out of place,
Sitting and stroking slowly at your ease
The spectres of your spider legs and knees,
And jingling spectral keys;
      Me, the spectre all forlorn,
      Tall and tattered, tossed and torn,
      Hollow of cheek, of aspect dreary!
      Domine, domine, miserere!
      But listen now as spirits can,
      Spirit of the sacristan!

A long, long time ago,
When you were sacristan,
A wheezy white-haired man,
Who fluttered to and fro
Through the church shadows after prayers,
Or perching on the belfry stairs,
Looked like a big black moth against the light
Of such a moon as shineth here to-night,—
When you were in the land of life, old ghost,
But wrinkled, blind, and deaf as any post,
I was a fine young spark of twenty-one,
Airing my merry beauty in the sun!
Ringlets were curling on my back,
My eyes were bright, my beard was black,
My lips were juicy, and beneath
Sparkled two rows of ivory teeth;
And everywhere I went, by day or night,
The women smiled and tingled with delight.
I clad myself, that all the fair might see,
Like to a blossom-laden apple tree;
I oiled my hair, I gave moustache a twirl,
I rouged my cheeks, powdered my teeth with pearl,
Then, with the air of corsair kings afloat,
 The arm-sweep of a king, I drank red wine;

And, in the secret of my chamber, wrote,
On many a pink embroidered little note,
    Petrarchan sonnets, which I wrote out fine,
That she might read, perchance, and smile on me—
        La Belle Dame Sans Mercy.

At the Duke's court, despite my admiration,
        Her charms made no sensation,
Although she was, the Duke himself admitted,
        Pleasing and subtle-witted.
Stuff! she was frivolous and narrow,—
Wit? with the brains of a she-sparrow!
        But, ah! the witty eyes;
  The ringlets shining golden as they shook;
The soft, soft tinkling laughter; and the wise
    Half innocent, half crafty look,
Wherewith, with small white finger fluttering gay
To tap your hand, she spake your heart away.
Her lips were sweet *bon mots*, her eyes a pun,
    Her cheeks were sarcasms mocking one to bliss;
And she would give her little glove in fun
    The sweetest of all epigrams—a kiss;
Well, for the rest, though older, bolder, colder,
She scarcely reached my shoulder—

A sweetling pale, too delicate to be human,
A little white mouse of a woman!

What wonder, then, that there, 'mong beauties tall,
And plump, and proud, she wandered lost and small?
And small she was indeed, though sweet,—so sweet,
From little shining head to tiny feet!
And, even as a small doe cropping flowers,
She minced between her teeth this speech of ours,
Till it was small and full of honey-juice,
     And fitted for her use.
And there it was! When hidden quite among
The flounced and furbelowed and flimsy throng,
She seemed so meek, so tiny, so unsinning,
I smiled, and dreamed she would be easy winning;
  For I was passing comely, as I thought,
And, further, gilded with a little gold;
  But, ah! for wealth and glitter she cared nought,
And as for love,—now mark me!—she was *cold.*

  Cold, ancient comrade—yes!
Not cold, though, to her poodle or her dress;
Not cold to the Court scandal and its sweets;
Not cold to ragged hunger in the streets;

21

Not cold to deep and noticeable grief
  Or gladness, whatsoe'er the rank and place of it;
Not cold unto the world; and, to be brief,
  Not even cold to me upon the face of it.
You take me? Warm as fire
  To whatsoever nice sensation chose
  To hover 'neath her nose,
Begging her eyes to pity or admire:
Not cold to gracious notice from the Duke;
Not cold entirely to my passionate look;
Not cold unto the dish that she was eating;
Not cold unto the friend whom she was meeting;
Not cold when hearing of your pain or strife;
  Not cold to kindly hint or savage comment;
  Not cold to aught she looked on, for the moment,
But cold to all the earth, for lasting life.

  So, though so sweet and small, as I have stated,
She seemed less charmed than I anticipated,
When, perfumed, powdered, pale, and hungry-eyed,
I followed in her silken train, and sighed.
When on my knee I gave her lily or rose,
  Oh, friend! to see her smiles and happy flushes!
To see her hold the gift up to her nose,

And flutter, till the bliss broke out in blushes!
But plague! ay, plague upon the wanton head!
      Whate'er you did or said,
Whate'er you placed before her peerless eyes,
Within her little bosom would arise
But one emotion, still the same—SURPRISE!
For lily or rose to smell, for book to read,
For the fresh glimpses of the woody mead,
For peeps in spring-tide at a sparrow's nest,
For peeps all seasons at a bleeding breast,
For compliment, praise, sorrow, wrath, admonishment,
      Her answer was—ASTONISHMENT!

    Even as a bee a rose's sweetness rifles,
She played with life, and sipped it best in trifles,
Nor took too greedy draughts of grief or pleasure,
But, slowly tasting, had of both her measure,
Since her small heart discovered deep enjoyment,
Her small brain amplest action and employment,
In delicately hovering on the brink
Of earnest, seeing others plunge and sink.
Thus, floating on the tide where'er it went,
Where'er it chose to carry her content,
She found for ever something here and there

Supremely sweet and fair,
Which for the minute occupied the whole
　　Of body and of soul,
And though she tripped divinely on the border
　Of folly, could be wicked in a way,
Keeping her little heart in icy order,
　So that it never tempted her astray.
And, mark: had I but known the way to win it,
And had I chosen just the proper minute,
Her heart, though neither amorous nor warm,
Might have been won by storm;
But, just as I approached her on the tide
Of faces, and she raised her hands, and cried,
　With blush divine and flutter of amaze,
'Oh, what a sweet young man!'
　Some other novelty drew off her gaze.—
　　But listen still as spirits can,
　　Spirit of the sacristan.

Now, when I made my passionate profession,
　With eyes serene she criticised my dress,
Peeped at my face, blushing at its expression,
　And smiling so divinely, you would guess
Her little mind was busy all the time

With sentiments sublime.
Then as my speech more passionate-languaged grew,
Fuller of feelings exquisite and choice,

And the full heart was thrilling in the voice,
Tears gathered quickly in her eyes of blue;
And then she noticed suddenly the fact
That my fine voice had husky grown and cracked,
By an accursèd draught caught through a door,
At the Duke's ball a night or two before.
And, ah! she trembled, fluttering and panting,
  While on my knees I fell, with voice that broke,
Urging me on divinely, and half granting
My boon with an astonishment enchanting,
  And thinking—in how thick a voice I spoke!
And when I paused, she thoughtfully perused me,
  And fluttering from my side, grew icy cold;
Then, softening to sweet sorrow, she refused me,—
      Because I had caught cold!

These women! never to be made out!
    Spirit of the sacristan!
The prologue of the business was played out,
    My vanity was paid out,
  But listen, ancient one, as spirits can.

First, by the cinders rescued from the flame
That roasted sweet St. Lawrence, by the blest

Toenails of Blois, by clippings from the same,
By the red nipples of St. Jonquil's breast,
By rags of St. Augustine's chemisette,
     Still odorous with her sweat,
By relics down below, by saints above,
I swear that I had loved as few men love!
Instead of seeking out the usual cure,
In lips more willing sweet, I grew demure,
Lost appetite, avoided all friends' faces,
Cried like a babe in solitary places,
Spilt in hot tears the wine I tippled nightly,
  Neglected dress, and cared not to be clean,
Till in the end a figure more unsightly
     Was nowhere to be seen.
Then, friend, between the liquor and the woe,
  My wits began to wander, memory failed me,
My brain was going—I could feel it go—
     And horrid dreams assailed me:
Then (while the friends and gossips deemed I lay
Butchered and dead in some untrodden way)
For human company and speech unfit,
  I sought, outside the town, the Swines' society,
And there the weathercock of my weak wit
     Turned suddenly to Piety!

Tall and tattered, tossed and torn,
Ragged and bare, and all forlorn,
With beard unkempt upon my breast unclean,
Hair matted on my shoulders,
Behold me—changed from what I once had been,
A sight to amaze beholders!
Sitting where swine resort, I shared
Their husks, and smote my bosom bared,
And prayed and prayed both day and night
To all the saints with all my might,
For heaven athirst, of life full weary,
Domine, domine, miserere!
But listen on as spirits can,
Spirit of the sacristan.

Here, in the city, spent in those days
His pious and morose days,
A long and lantern-featured Carmelite,
As melancholy as the garb he wore,
Famed for his horror of all lewd delight,
Unspiritual feats at dead of night,
And for a vow that he had made—no more
To look on water, till his days were o'er;
A grimy man, with eye like any hawk,

Sententious, hating talk.

To him I bent my steps one evening late,

12

Half naked, hairy, foul, and sick for food,
And found him standing at the convent gate,
   Moodily scowling underneath his hood.
And after *benedicite* was uttered
There was a pause; and, while I shook and fluttered,
He noticed, with complaisance and amaze,
My dirty dress and my lack-lustre gaze,
My skeleton frame, and hollow sunken cheek,
         Wild hair, and beard antique.
Then, gripping at his robe, I questioned greedily
   How such a poor unfortunate as I
Might purchase for his spirit, and most speedily,
   A place among the blesséd in the sky?

         With wild anticipation
The hair upon my hapless body bristled,
As, pursing up his lips, gravely he whistled;
         And with deliberation
Widening the hawk's eye, deeplier black than soot,
         Eyed me from head to foot.
Long did he meditate in silence, eyeing me
As if I were a brute, and he were buying me;
And when at last he had appraised me fully,
He stopped, and whispered coolly,

'Be of good cheer, my son!
Thy place among the holy shall be won,
And in a speedy manner, if unpleasant ·
We are in want of a new SAINT at present,-
A place not easily nor lightly had;
        But in my estimation,
You are a very likely sort of lad
        To fill the situation.'

        Listen on, as spirits can,
        Spirit of the sacristan.
Ere long a rumour travelled up and down,
And grew from street to street, and stirred the town,
That grace at last had fallen in a shower
        Upon the holy Brothers Carmelite,
Ev'n in the figure of a saint, whose power
        Made even faith turn white,
And whom a brother found one evening late
Dropped as from heaven at the cloister gate,
Pale as the dead, naked and bare completely,
And praying in strange tongues, and smiling sweetly.
Wonder of wonders!—when these holy men
    Bare him within, he frowning turned from bread,
Nor had he taken bite or sup since then,

But sat apart, with ashes on his head,
Full of deep rapture, in a dripping cell,
    While rats and lizards crawled on head and breast;
And whoso, being sick, approached, was well,
    And whoso filled his lap with gifts, was blest.
Wonders!—ay, miracles! Rich and poor came near!
Fine ladies in their coaches, prince and peer;
    The ill, the well, the youthful, and the hoary:
While I, now dimly shaping my insanity
        Into a ghastly vanity,
        Went starving up to glory.

Ha, ha! And yet you question, my old friend,
The bodily bliss of such a hungry end.
But take, I pray, into consideration
        The spiritual exaltation,
        The great and beautiful goal
That body was employed to earn for soul;
    And now, if still you think I did amiss,
And should have ta'en my fill of fleshly passion,
    Lean over your old ears, and answer this—
Who, when the wondrous Saint had grown the fashion,
Was first to kneel unto him on her knee?—
        La Belle Dame Sans Mercy!

Now, hold your breath and hearken! While
  I sat upon my bed and prayed,
With glazéd eye and vacant smile,
    Nor saw nor heeded those who paid
    Their vows before me in the shade,
Suddenly from my trance I started:
    The spell seemed broken; through my brain
Strange whispers from the world there darted,—
  My heart was thick with a strange pain;
      And I was 'ware
Of a sweet voice that filled the air!
And of a rustling dress, and of a smell
More pleasing than the odour of the cell;
And, darkly stirred from my ecstatic doze,
  I yawned and rolled my black eyes round to see,
  And, lo! a slight shape kneeling close to me,
Holding a smelling-bottle to her nose;
      And at the sight
My eyeballs seemed to burst and burn with light!
My skin was like a snake's, wrinkled and curled,
  I felt the blood like lava froth and roll;
Yet still I sat as stone, while all the world
  Came back upon my soul!

O God! to see her there!
The tearful face, the golden hair!
To sicken in the perfumes of her dress,
To drink her breath, to feel her loveliness,
To see the rapturous worship in her eyes,
True (for that minute) as the changeless skies,
   To feel, to smell, to burn, to see,
To hear her musical accents fall and rise,
     Praying to me, to me!
And there we sat in the dim dusk, alone,
  She looking down, and pale with passionate prayer,
Till at her ear I made a ghastly groan,
  And, looking up, she met my frozen stare;
And then, with fingers in her palms compressed,
  Screaming and fluttering, gasping at the air,
    Fell fainting on my breast!

Now all the world was mine! I could not think!
But to hold tight my burthen, and to drink
  Her beauty like wild wine, was all my care;
Or dipping in the ashes and the sands,
Slowly to let them trickle through my hands
  Upon the powdered face and scented hair,
And laugh, and laugh in ecstasy divine,

Feeling the flutter of her heart on mine;
Or tearing at her boddice, with dark mouth

To kiss her snowy breasts and leave the stains,
And drink the joy, as though I slaked my drouth
　　Out of her purple veins!

Even as we sat, behold! a flash of light,
　Then thunder, following soon;
And, as the tempest deepened through the night,
　She wakened from her swoon;
While the pale meteors flickered through the place,
　Frightening the rats and lizards to their lair.
Great joy was mine to gaze into her face,
　And drink her breath, and toy with her soft hair,
　　And feel she could not scream,
Nor stir, but only lie in a wild dream,
And look into my eyes, and feel my breath,
　While the light flickered and the thunder rolled;
Until I knew that she had swooned to death,
　　Because she grew so cold!

　　Ere morning, at her side,
The Saint stretched out his skeleton limbs and died;
The rapture of that night was far too rare
　　For one so blest to bear;
But afterwards 't was made a tale of wonder,

That late at evening, when the little dame
Confessed her sins before the Saint, there came
A terrible Fiend, with lightning and with thunder,
Intending for the soul o' the Saint that night
    To risk a last fierce fight;
But being overthrown, of course, entirely
    By one whose sinless nature could defy him,
The Fiend had thereupon demolished direly
    The sinful dame close by him;
In sign of which the pious folk might note
Those stains like finger-marks upon her throat!

    You shiver, friend! He! he!
  Well, now my tale is told, you may repose,—
And, for the rest, there in the crypt you see
    My saintship—broken nose and turned-up toes!
    But, hark! that distant crowing,
Familiar, ancient ghost, to me and you!
The morn is breaking. Cock-a-doodle-doo!
    'T is time that we were going!

THE EXILES OF OONA.

(NORTH COAST, 18—.)

I.

ON THE HILL-SIDE.

SO still he sat upon the mountain-side,
  The white cloud rested on him there, and mingled
Its dew-breath with the moisture on his eyelids;

So still and gray, the rainy light played on him,
As on an antique statue hewn in stone—
A worn old boulder, not an old man breathing;

So still, the ancient sheep-dog at his feet
Rose up, and placed its cold nose in his palm,
And gazed upon him, wondering he stirred not;

So still, he noted not the dreamy stranger,
Who, breathing hard after the steep ascent,
Stood close at hand, and musing looked upon him.

This old man's heart was not on the hill-side,
Nor with the flying cloud, nor on the heather,
That stained the dark hill-side like bloody footprints;

He could not see the flowing of the shadows,
The palpitating light; he could not hear
The brook sing, nor the wind blow, nor the shepherd

Shouting afar off to the mountain echoes;
He could not feel the touch of wind and cloud;
Yet all these things had portion with his sorrow.

His eyes were fixed upon the still vale lying
Beneath him, on the space beside the pine-wood,
And on the gray deer twinkling in its shadow.

And yet these things he saw not, but saw visions:
The blue peat-smoke curling from human dwellings,
The matron spinning on the clean red threshold,

And down the dale the kilted huntsman, standing
With chin thrust forward, watching, while the hills
Echoed the sharp peal of his smoking gun.

Yea, all the things he heard were visions also,—
The humming of the wheel, the low of kine,
The sheep-dog barking, and the sheep-bell tinkling.

So still, so still, he sat in meditation,
The sheep-dog watched with dumb and piteous eyes,
And the dark stranger looked, and came no nearer;

And neither knew his eyes were moist and dim,
Because he heard the cry of little children
Filling the dale where little children were not.

Till, setting hand upon the old man's shoulder,
The stranger murmured, in the Gaelic speech,
'Can this be Adam Hart that I behold?'

When, looking up under his twitching eyelids,
The old man saw a bearded, bronzéd face,
Wherein much thought had hardened into wrinkles;

A face familiar with the wind and water,
A worn companion of the ocean tempest,
And yet the face of one in life's mid-season.

And long and wearily, with querulous wonder
The old man gazed; then said in a low voice,
'Your face is strange, and yet you seem to know me.'

'Know you!' the stranger echoed, laughing sadly;
'Not Oona yonder, with his cloud-cap on,
Not the salt sea beyond, is more familiar.

'Am I so changed with piping tunes to Fortune,
So twisted to the likeness of the world,
That even my old master hath forgot me?

'Does the first face I meet, returning homeward,
Look thus upon me, with no smile of greeting?
Has Adam Hart forgotten Hector Stuart?'

Then as one smitten sudden by a sunbeam,
Dazzled and blinded, Adam cried aloud,
'Hector!' and trembled like a breaking wave;

And gripped the strong hand with his feeble fingers,
And rubbed his eyes, and looked again, still doubting,
And moved his lips, but spoke not, breathing deep.

‘ Why, see !’ cried Hector, while the hound smelt round
   him,
’ And looked into his face as if in greeting,
‘ Why, see, old Fingal’s memory is better !

‘ He knows his ancient playmate on these hills ;
   Though ten long years have passed, he has a welcome,
   A kiss too !’ for the old hound licked his fingers.

Then for a space the eyes of Adam Hart
Dimmed their weak orbs on Hector, till at last
His voice found speech in accents faint and broken.

‘ Hector ! alive !—a wraith among the wraiths
   Of the old clachan ! Now indeed I know you ;
   The voice grows on me, ay, and the face haunts me.

‘ Welcome !—and yet how can I give you welcome ?
   My heart aches, Hector. I am old and broken ;—
   Ah, God ! all things are changed since you departed.

‘ I am the grave of him you knew. At times
   It seems that I am harder than these rocks,
   Surrounded but by mist and hollow voices.

'Useless and feeble, here I linger yet,
　As animals linger on, content, and never
　Smiling as happy human folk can smile.

'Yet welcome, welcome to a weary place,
　And to a weary bosom. You have heard—
　You know—things are not as they were of old?'

'Ay, Adam,' Hector answered, bitterly,
　Glancing into the valley at his feet,
'I have heard much, but there is more to hear.

'Yet fear not; nothing now can quite appal me;
　I am too used to the rough stabs of men;
　The world is full of devils—men must fight them.'

Clear were his accents as the plover's crying,
And fierce and strong he stood, but his keen eyes
Peered upon Adam with a questioning hunger.

And Adam knew the thing he dared not ask,
And murmured, looking downward, 'Have you seen
　　　them?
The old folk?' And the eyes of Hector kindled.

'Nay, but they live!' he cried, and gripped the arm
Of Adam, searching in his eyes for answer.
'They live? they live?' And Adam answered, 'Surely!'

Then tears came, which the strong man dashed aside,
Tears through whose mist the old man's weary shape,
And rocks, and trees, and clouds, swam phantom-like;

And for a moment like a broken reed
He trembled there; then as a lion's mane
Shakes off the dew, he dashed away the weakness,

Saying, 'God has not lied upon the waters!
The wind, the waves, the sea-birds, cried they lived;
It is enough—I ask no more of God.

'Oh, dawn by dawn rose up across the greenness
Of the blank sea, and I was looking eastward,
Hither to Scotland—hither to the home;

'And not a star by night but said they lived;
And when the white moon walked alone above me,
I felt that it was shining on their faces.

21

'And in the smooth sea, over snipboard leaning,
 I saw the lines of mountains and of pine-woods,
 And seemed to hear the rush of mountain torrents;

'And the sails' creaking overhead at night
 Was like the wind's sough in the tall tree-tops;
 And the wave plashing on the vessel's side

'Was full of Highland sounds; and when I trode
 The deck, my step was proud, my head erect,
 Because I seemed to walk upon the heather.

'It is enough, I say, to know they live;
 The rest is easy—they will smile upon me,
 I shall be near them, I shall close their eyes.'

Stilly the old man listened; his dim eyes
Roamed heavenward with no look of vacant worship,
And, suddenly, his face went white as wool,

His dim eye flamed under his wrinkled forehead,
And fiercely with his staff he smote the ground,
And cried, 'There are more bitter things than dying!

'Better be foul with dust, be food for worms,
 Better be food for foul crows on the hill-side,
 Than see again the things that I have seen.

'I say there is no refuge from these things,
 But sleep like that! My heart cries up at God!
 How can He sit so still and see it all?'

Then, as the black wind passes from a lake,
And leaves the quiet surface merely troubled,
His anger faded, and his voice grew weaker.

'Heaven help us all, alas, we need some help!
Why, sometimes, when I sit and muse alone,
My hand grasps thus, like one that seeks a knife.

'Ay, and such murder were less black, I swear,
Than is that other murder base men pardon,—
The poison dropped into the poor man's bowl,

'The draining of the heart's blood drop by drop,
To feed the red deer and the flying fowl,
Making us carrion for the beasts, though living.

'O Hector, where the little children came
To lisp the English tongue at these old knees,
The sportsman's dogs loll out red tongues and bay;

'And where the Highland lassie drew her water,
The moor-hen builds her clumsy nest of sedge,
And bloody hands see that she does not hunger;

'And where the old gray men and snooded matrons
Gathered to hear the wandering preacher preach,
The horned buck leads his dun herds, silent-footed.

‘ And bloody heather grows upon the threshold,
 And on the hearth the bitch-stag bears her litter,
 And not a human sound disturbs the stillness.

'And yet the clouds pass, and the sun is shining,
And the hills keep their seats, and GOD sees all,
Who made the bonnie world for men and women.'

And Hector answered not, but cast around him
A gaze like that cast by a shipwrecked sailor
Over a lonely waste of sky and water.

And neither spake again.   The old man gripped
His staff, and led the way across the hill,
The old hound running slowly at his heels;

While Hector Stuart followed, with his eyes
Searching the landmarks of his youth, and ever
Seeing some bitter change as in a dream.

Sweet was the air, that afternoon of autumn,
For day was going gently o'er the hills,
Lifting the loose hair with a last moist breathing :

Westward, between the hills, the sinking sun
Burned like a chrysolite on one smooth sweep
Of ocean, turning it to gleams of fire ;

While overhead the blue west turned to amber,
Liquid and golden, underneath the shadow
Of one long line of purple-rimméd vapour.

Nearer, on either hand, arose the hills,
Clothed with the soft and mossy tints of autumn,
Blue, gray, and purple, flecked with velvet shadows;

The boulder gray in sunset, and, still nearer,
The boulder's shade; the golden tippéd pine-wood,
And, underneath, the shadow of the pine-wood;

And as the sunlight travelled on the hill-side,
The fallow and the brood-deer with their shadows
Followed in mottled swarms from gleam to gleam;

And from their track the clumsy partridge flew,
Whirring and screaming, and the red grouse rose
And winged its way down to the running brook.

It was a scene that seemed at peace with GOD,
Beautiful with His beauty, strange and sweet,
And not a sound broke on the hush of sunset,

Save the breeze breathing, and that half-heard murmur
The hills make to each other when they feel
The burden of God's stillness heavy on them.

Not yet at peace with that sweet stillness throbbed
The hearts of those over the hill-side wending,
With twisted shadows lengthening from the west.

And Adam looked not around him as he walked,
But pulled his bonnet o'er his wrinkled brow
And gazed upon the ground through the white hair

Blown in his eyes by the moist mountain breeze;
And the old hound leaped not nor made a sound,
And seemed to know the sorrow of his master.

But Hector Stuart looked toward the ocean,
And finding hope there, brightened thitherward,
And trode with lighter footstep on the heather.

From mossy ridge to ridge they passed in silence,
While dimlier, darklier, fell the dewy twilight,
And then at last descended to the valley.

Then on by rocky paths they journeyed slowly,
Winding their way 'neath dismal crags and boulders,
Until they reached the shadow of the pine-wood.

25

Here, pausing, Adam pointed through the twilight,
And said, 'This is my home.' And Hector gazed,
But saw no sign of human habitation.

Only at intervals the dim black square,
The heap of stones, the moss-wrapt threshold-stone,
Showing where human dwellings late had been;

And here and there among the growing grass
The wild potato mingled up with weeds,
Yet blooming, tilled no more by human hands;

And on the sun-side of a little hillock
The wind stirred on a little patch of greenness—
A piteous little patch of growing corn.

Then Hector stood upon the threshold-stone,
Saying, 'Were I not hard, my heart would break ;
But wind and wave have done their duty, Adam.

'Why, on this very place my mother sat,
At sunset hour, and held me up to see
Her strong man bounding lightly from the hills.

'Desolate, desolate, all desolate !
No touch of hands, no sound of happy voices !
Speak, Adam ; lift the burden from my heart.

'I cannot hunger on in silence longer—
I must hear all : pour out, yea, drop by drop,
As if it were my heart's blood you were pouring.

So speaking, he distinguished in the twilight
A rude mud shieling, worn with wind and weather,
And round the walls the tall dark flagweed growing ;

And on the roof grew slimy grass and weeds,
The wild leek, and the wallflower, tufts of corn;
And in the midst a thin she-goat stood browsing.

'Enter,' said Adam Hart, 'and you shall hear
All that my tongue can tell you of our story,
The woe, the bitter cup that we have drunk;

'And here this night take shelter, if you will,
And let my speech prepare your heart to suffer
The things your eyes shall look upon at dawn.'

II.

THE KIRKYARD OF GLEN OONA.

LIKE one whose spirit evil dreams have troubled,
  Haggard and weary, Hector Stuart wakened,
After a heavy sleep on sheaves of straw ;

And, rolling wild eyes round the dusky chamber,
Unlit by any window-pane or loophole,
Knew by the chill o' the air that it was dawn.

' You have slept sound,' said Adam, stooping o'er him.
And Hector, with a bitter laugh and hollow,
Cried, ' Fair or stormy weather, 't is our way !

' But I have dreamt—GOD keep me from such dreams !
I saw it all—I heard—'t was clear as waking—
The terror and the sorrow of that story.

' The women's shrieks are in my ears; I feel
  The white woe of their faces; I behold
  Fire and the fiends of hell devour the dwellings !'

Then, rising up, he drew his plaid around him,
And stepped across the threshold, where the dawn
Fell like a silver trouble on his features,

And, drinking in the air with swelling nostrils,
Doffed to the sunrise, and beheld the vapours
Clothing the hills and steaming in the valleys,

While, overhead, the lift from gray to blue
Kindled, and white light deepened from the east,
And far off faintly barked a huntsman's hound.

' Desolate! desolate!' he cried aloud,
 Full bitterly; 'no cries of little bairns,
 No happy voices welcoming the sunrise;

' But, cold and gray, dawn drops into the silence,
 Startling the deer and wild fowl from their lairs,
 To make the lonely desolation deeper.'

Then Adam called him in, and set before him
Oat-bread and whisky; and he ate and drank,
Feeding the sheep-dog moodily from his palm;

And when the meal was over, Adam took
His staff, and whistled to the dog, and left
The shieling, followed slowly by the seaman.

Northward they turned, and ankle-deep in dew,
Walked in the dusky shadow of the mountains,
Then through the chillness of a dripping wood;

Whence issuing, they came upon the brink
Of a dark water, bottomed with black slate,
And girt around by mountains steep and sunless.

There all was silent as a dead man's heart,
Chill, still, and sombre, and a filmy rain
Was shaken from a dim and cloudless sky;

While the dark water shimmered, and thin waves
Broke with no sound upon the lonely shore,
O'er which the wild black ouzel whirled and screamed.

Then Hector crossed himself, and shivered, saying,
' Well might the ancient women of the clachan
Christen this loch the Water of the Dead !

' 'T is stiller than the frozen seas ; 't is drearer
Than a dead calm with rain on the mid-ocean !
Why came we hither ?   Whither are we bound ?'

Even as he spake, dead silentness was broken
By a strange music, echoing far away,—
A murmur like a wind, yet deeper, louder.

'Hark!' cried the old man, and the sound grew clearer,
And echoes faintly leaped from hill to hill,
Dying afar off on the thymy peaks ;

And clearer grew the music, till, at last,
Distinct, though faint, an ancient Scottish air
Came floating melancholy o'er the water.

'The pipes!' cried Hector, holding up his hand
Against his ear, and hearkening open-mouthed,
'The pipes! They play the Sorrow of Lochaber!'

2.i

Even like a ghostly melody by spirits
Woven, and wafted faintly o'er the waters
That flow between us and the shores that lie

Behind the horizon of our mutual sorrows,
Over the lonely lake that music floated,
A plaintive trouble in the heart of silence,—

While the day grew, and still the rain was shaken
Out of the brightening lift, and on the hill-tops
The filmy wreaths of vapour thinned and lifted,

Showing the stony peaks and alps untrodden,
The torrents downward flashing through the spray,
The runlet glistening silver through the shadows.

Then sunrise, glistening faintly o'er the peaks,
Fell moist and slant into the lake beneath,
And where the rays fell clearest, far away

In the mid-water, moving very slowly,
With measured stroke of dripping oars, a boat
Appeared out of the fading mists of morning;

And clearer, louder, from the boat was wafted
The plaintive air, the Sorrow of Lochaber,
Aching upon the heart-strings of the hearers;

And as the boat drew nearer, and the music
Grew clearer yet and louder, they who watched
Beheld a sad and silent companie:

The boatmen hanging heads and pulling slow,
And men and women sitting sadly round them,
And all the men bareheaded to the sunrise;

And stretched along the stern a silent shape,
Covered from head to foot with sombre plaid,
And by its side a white-haired priest, who prayed;

And at its head the Piper stood erect,
Gazing across the waters, playing softly,
Lochaber, and Lochaber, and Lochaber!

Then Adam raised the bonnet from his brow,
And drooped his gray head, saying, 'Blest be he
Whom they are bearing to his happy sleep!

'I have no tear for him, the blessèd dead;
My tears are for the living, whose sad eyes
Must close beyond the sunset, on strange shores;

'How shall they sleep in peace apart from dust
Of kindred? How shall man or woman rest
Out of the quiet shadow of these hills?

' Better have stabbed with bloody huntsman's knife
Man, wife, and bairn! better with gun and hounds
Have hunted them for sport across the heather !

' Then had their end been sweeter, for their eyes
  Had closed among the hills where they were born,
  And they had slumbered in familiar places !'

And nearer yet and nearer came the boat,
And clearer yet and clearer grew the air,—
Lochaber, and Lochaber, and Lochaber!

And those who sat within the boat were plainer,
Women and men, a ragged companie,
Each with a band of black around the arm;

But most were very old, yea, ancient men,
White-haired and wrinkled, leaning on their staves,
And toothless crones with visionary eyes;

And some were crooning in a thin low voice
A Gaelic chant, and counting over beads,
With blank eyes fixéd on the space where God

Dwelt as a misty trouble; and a few
Kept time with feeble lips to the sad music
Made by the gray old piper in the stern.

Then, quickening oars, the rowers ran the boat
Into a narrow cove, and touched the shore,
And one by one the pale-faced mourners landed,—

Old women leaning on their weeping daughters,
And ancient shepherds on their sons; the rowers
Helping the feeblest gently up the shore.

And one there was, old, old, who could not see,
But, stooping double, leaned upon his staff,
And had an old, old sheep-dog for his guide.

'Follow!' said Adam, while the mourners wended
Along that silent land, and slowly entered
The still green darkness of a little wood;

And they who watched were 'ware of others coming
From east and west, by mountain-path and valley,
All making for the wood, and sadly meeting;

And, while the gray old piper led the mourners,
Tenderly playing, from the east and west
Came other players, leading other mourners;

Till hill, and vale, and water rang, and voices
Took up the gentle strain in accents broken—
Lochaber, and Lochaber, and Lochaber!

And Hector Stuart, following Adam Hart,
Came to the wood, and peering through the trees,
Beheld the kirkyard of the clan within:

A desolate place, where rough graves, rudely heapen,
Gathered like waves, with rocks and stones between,
And in the midst a Runic cross quaint-carven;

And there around an open tomb they gathered,
Ragged and homeless, while the gray-haired priest
Cried shrilly the sad service for the dead;

27

Till, his voice ceasing, once again the pipes
Played softly, and across that weary crew
There ran the blunted moan of hearts o'erladen.

Then Adam whispered, 'Blest is he they bury!
For yonder in the haven waits the ship,
And ere the sun sets twice the ship will sail;

'And all these souls will gather on her decks,
Heart-broken, bitter; gazing, young and old,
While Scotland fades into the waste of water.'

Silent they stood, each gazing on the dust
Of kindred,—on the well-belovéd ones
Whom they should never lie beside in slumber.

It was a sight that withered up the heart,
To see these old, old faces, pinched and tearless,
Those quivering heads, those hands strained tight together;

To mark the woe of women, and the heartache
Of ancient men, all human, and all wearing
The piteous justification of gray hairs!

Then one cried, 'GOD, my GOD, I want to die!
The sweetest of my bairns are gathered here:
How should I breathe the air across the sea?'

And then another answered, 'He knows best!'
And yet I would His sleep were on my een;
He knows that I must die if ta'en from home.'

And yet another said, 'Our bairns are young,
And care not; they are strong, and love to roam :
Let them depart in peace, if we may stay.

'This is the glen where wife and I were born,
These are the hills we know, this is the place
Where we had hoped to slumber side by side.'

And at his words, his wife, an ancient dame,
Groaned loud, and sobbed, and lifted up her arms,
And, praying, fell upon her knees beside him.

Then once again the priest brake out in prayer,
Solemn and piteous; and the place was hushed,
And the day brightened, and the heaven grew clearer :

And on a steep crag, overhead, behold !
Huge antlers glimmered, then a mighty stag
Rose slowly, the red Monarch of those wilds,

And, while behind him followed harts and hinds,
Brood-deer and fallow, gathering swarm on swarm,
He gazed with bloodshot eye on his dominions;

Then vanished as a mist, with all his people,
In silence; while the Exiles prayed bareheaded,
And, faint and low, the pipers played Lochaber!

Lochaber! and Lochaber! and Lochaber!

HAHON.

HAHON of Thule, ere he died,
  Summoned a priest to his bed-side.

'Ho, priest,' he said, with glazéd e'e,
'What comfort canst thou give to me?'

The young priest, with a timorous mouth,
Told of the new gods of the South,—

Of Mary mother and her Child,
And holy saints with features mild;

Of those who hate and those who love,
Of hell below and heaven above.

Then Hahon laughed full loud and shrill—
'Serve thy puny gods who will!

''Neath braver gods my star was born;
How should I pray to things I scorn?'

Then, calling to his henchman red,
' Slit me the throat o' the priest,' he said ;

' His red heart's blood shall flow before,
As gracious sacrifice to Thor !

' Bring me my mighty drinking-cup !
With fiery wine now fill it up !'

Then, though so faint his life's blood ran,—
' Let me die standing, like a man !'

He swore, and staggered to his legs,
And drained the goblet to the dregs.

' Skaal be to the gods !' he said—
His great heart burst, and he was dead !

CELTIC MYSTICS.

I.

I F thou art an Angel,
   Who hath sent thee,
O Phantasy, brooding
Over my pale wife's sleeping?
   In the darkness
   I am listening
For the rustle of thy robe;
Would I might feel thee breathing,
Would I might hear thee speaking,
Would I might only touch thee
   By the hand!

   She is very cold,
   My wife is very cold,
   Her eyes are withered,

Her breath is dried like dew,—
The sound of my weeping
    Disturbeth her not.
Thy shadow, O Phantasy,
    Lieth like moonlight
    Upon her features,
And the lines of her mouth
    Are very sweet.

    In the night
I heard my pale wife moaning,
    Yet did not know
    What made her afraid.
    My pale wife said,
   'I am very cold,'
And shrank away from thee,
Though I saw thee not;
And she kissed me and went to sleep,
And gave a little start upon my arm
When thou camest near
    And touchedst her!

    What art thou?
    Art thou an Angel?

Or art thou only
The chilly night-wind,
Stealing downward
From the regions where the sun
Dwelleth alone with his shadow
On a waste of snow?
Art thou the water or earth?
Or art thou the scented air?
Or art thou only
An apparition
Made by the mist
Of mine own eyes weeping?

She is very cold,
My wife is very cold!
I will kiss her,
And the silver-haired mother will kiss her,
And the little children will kiss her;
And then we will wrap her warm,
And hide her in a hollow space;
And the house will be empty
Of thee, O Phantasy,
Cast on the unhappy household
By the strange white clay.

Much I marvel, O Phantasy,
　　That one so gentle,
　　So sweet, when living,
Should cast a shadow so huge as thine;
　　For, lo ! thou loomest
　　Upward and heavenward,
　　Hiding the sunlight,
　　Blackening the snow,
And the pointing of thy finger
　　Fadeth afar away
On the sunset-tinged edges,
Where Time and mortal vision perish,
Where Man's company ends,
And God's loneliness begins.

II.

THE VISION.

A ND sitting by her side, worn out with weeping,
    Behold, I fell to sleep, and had a vision,
Wherein I heard a wondrous voice intoning :

Crying aloud, 'The Master on His throne
Openeth now the seventh seal of wonder,
And beckoneth back the angel men name Death ;

'And at His feet the filmy terror kneeleth,
  Breathing not; and the Lord doth look upon him,
  Saying, "Thy wanderings, dear Cain, are ended.

'"To thee, O Cain, I gave in the beginning
  The punishment of dealing out decay,
  And, lo! thou art the sweeter from thy labour.

' " Hie back into the City of the Chosen,
Where Abel is awaiting to embrace thee;
I need thee on the earth of men no longer." '

And there the dreamy angel sitteth silent,
Even at the silver gates of heaven,
Drowsily looking in on the Eternal,

And puts his silence among men no longer.

*

And at the bottom of a snowy mountain
I came upon a woman sorrow-thinned,
Whose voice was like the crying of a sea-gull,

Saying, ' O Death, Death, Death, come hither, hither;
And bring the corpse I seek for on thy bosom,
That I may close its eyelids and embrace it.

' I curse thee that I cannot look upon him!
I curse thee that I know not he is sleeping!
Yet know that he has vanished upon GOD!

'I laid my little girl upon a wood-bier,
And very sweet she seemed, and near unto me,
And putting flowers into her shroud was comfort.

'I put my silver mother in the darkness,
And kissed her, and was solaced by her kisses,
And set a stone, to mark the place, above her.

'And green, green were their quiet sleeping-places,
So green that it was pleasant to remember
That I and my tall man would sleep beside them.

'The closing of dead eyelids is not dreadful,
For comfort comes upon us when we close them,
And tears fall, and our sorrow grows familiar;

'And we can sit above them where they slumber,
And spin a dreamy pain into a sweetness,
And know indeed that we are very near them.

'But to stretch out empty arms is surely dreadful,
And to feel the horrid empty world is awful,
And bitter grow the silence and the distance.

'There is no space for grieving or for weeping;
No touch, no cold, no agony to strive with,
And nothing but a horror and a blankness.'

20

*

And, behold! I saw a woman in a mud-hut,
Raking the white spent embers with her fingers,
And fouling her bright hair with the white ashes;

And her mouth was very bitter with the ashes;
Her eyes with dust were blinded; and her sorrow
Sobbed in the throat of her like gurgling water.

And all around the voiceless hills were hoary,
And a red light scorched their edges; and above her
There was a soundless trouble of the cloud-reek.

'Whither, and, oh, whither,' said the woman,
'O Spirit of the Lord, hast thou conveyed them—
My little ones, my little son and daughter?

'For, lo! we wandered forth at early morning,
And winds were blowing round us, and their mouths
Blew rose-buds to the rose-buds, and their eyes

'Looked violets at the violets, and their hair

Made a sunshine in the sunshine, and their passing
Left a pleasure in the dewy leaves behind them;

'And suddenly my little son looked upward,
 And his eyes were dried like dew-drops; and his going
 Was like a blow of fire upon my face.

'And my little son was gone. My little daughter
 Looked round me for him, clinging to my vesture,
 But the LORD had blown him from me, and I knew it

'By the sign He gives the stricken that the lost one
 Lingers nowhere on the earth on hill or valley,
 Neither underneath the grasses or the tree-roots.

'And my shriek was like the splitting of an ice-reef,
 And I sank among my hair, and all my palm
 Was moist and warm where the little hand had filled it.

'Then I fled and sought him wildly hither—thither—
 Though I knew that he was stricken from me wholly
 By the token that the spirit gives the stricken.

'I sought him in the sunlight and the starlight,
 I sought him in the forests, and in waters
 Where I saw mine own pale image looking at me.

'And I forgot my little bright-haired daughter,
Though her voice was like a wild bird far behind me,
Till the voice ceased, and the universe was silent.

'And stilly, in the starlight, came I backward
To the forest where I missed him; and no voices
Brake the stillness as I stooped down in the starlight,

'And saw two little shoes filled up with dew,
And no mark of little footsteps any farther,
And knew my little daughter had gone also.'

*

The world was very quiet. Men in traffic
Cast looks over their shoulders; pallid seamen
Went wild to walk upon the decks alone;

And women barred their doors with bars of iron,
In the silence of the night; and at the sunrise
Shivered behind their husbandmen afield.

Only the children sported very stilly,
And grew paler and still paler, and drew closer
Unto their mothers as they wox the older.

I could not see a kirkyard near or far;
I thirsted for a green grave, and my vision
Was hungry for the white gleam of a tombstone.

But hearkening dumbly, ever and anon
I heard a cry out of a human dwelling,
And felt the cold wind of a lost one's going.

One struck a brother fiercely, and he fell,
And faded in a darkness; and that other
Tore his hair, and was afraid, and could not perish.

One struck his aged mother on the mouth,
And she vanished with a gray grief from her hearth-stone.
One melted from her bairn, and on the ground

The bairn lay smiling up, with pink curled fingers.
And many made a weeping among mountains,
And hid themselves in caverns, and were drunken.

And I heard a voice from out the beauteous earth,
Whose side rolled up from winter into summer,
Crying, 'I am grievous for my children.'

And I heard a voice from out the dreadful ocean,
Crying, ' Burial in the breast of me were better,
Yea, burial in the salt flags and green crystals.'

And I heard a voice from out the hollow ether
Saying, ' The thing ye cursed hath been abolished,—
Corruption, and decay, and dissolution !'

And the world shrieked, and the summer-time was bitter,
And men and women feared the air behind them,
And for lack of its green graves the world was hateful.

*

But beasts died; yea, the cattle in the yoke,
The milk-cow in the meadow, and the sheep,
And the dog upon the door-step; and men envied.

And birds died; yea, the eagle at the sun-gate,
The swan upon the waters, and the farm-fowl,
And the swallows on the house-tops; and men envied.

And reptiles; yea, the toad upon the road-side,
The slimy speckled snake among the grass,
The lizard on the ruin; and men envied.

The dog in lonely places cried not over
The body of his master; but it missed him,
And whined into the air, and died, and rotted.

And the traveller's horse lay swollen in the pathway,
And the blue fly fed upon it; but no traveller
Was there,—yea, not his footprint on the ground.

30

And the cat mewed in the midnight, and the blind
Gave a rustle, and the lamp burnt blue and faint,—
And the father's bed was empty in the morning.

And the mother fell to sleep beside the cradle,
Rocking it while she slumbered with her foot,
And wakened,—and the cradle there was empty.

I saw a two-years' child, and he was playing;
And he found a dead white bird upon the doorway,
And laughed, and ran to show it to his mother.

And the mother moaned, and clutched him, and was bitter,
And flung the dead white bird across the threshold,
And another white bird flitted round and round it,

And uttered a sharp cry, and twittered, and twittered,
And lit beside its dead mate, and grew busy,
Strewing it over with green leaves and yellow.

*

So far, so far to seek for were the limits
Of affliction; and men's terror grew a homeless
Terror, and a fatal sense of blankness.

There was no little token of distraction,
There was no visible presence of bereavement,
Such as the mourner easeth out his heart on.

There was no comfort of the slow farewell,
Nor gentle shutting of belovéd eyes,
Nor beautiful broodings over sleeping features.

There were no kisses on familiar faces,
No weaving of pure grave-clothes, no last pondering
Over the still wax cheeks and folded fingers.

There was no putting tokens under pillows,
There was no dreadful beauty slowly fading
From the vision, slowly fading into darkness,—

So slowly, that, when it doth vanish wholly,
The heart is ready with its tears and outlet,
And parting can be borne with, though so bitter.

There were no churchyard paths to walk on, thinking
How near the well-belovéd ones are lying;
There were no sweet green graves to sit and muse on,

Till grief should grow a summer meditation,
The shadow of the passing of an Angel,
And sleeping should seem easy and not cruel.

Nothing but wondrous parting and a blankness.

*

And I woke, and, lo! the burthen was uplifted,
And I prayed within the chamber where she slumbered,
And my tears flowed fast and free, but were not bitter.

I eased my heart three days by watching near her,
And made her pillow sweet with scent and flowers,
And could bear at last to put her in the darkness.

And I heard the kirk-bells ringing very slowly,
And the priests were in their vestments; and the earth
Dripped awful on the hard wood, yet I bore it.

And I cried, 'O unseen Sender of corruption!
I bless Thee for the wonder of Thy mercy,
Wherein Thou helpest us to lose our loved ones.

'I bless Thee for the change and for the comfort,
The fixéd face, shut eyes, and waxen fingers ;
For sleeping, and for silence and corruption.

'I bless Thee that she slumbers underneath me,
I bless Thee for the place that will be cheerful
When the winter of mine agony is over.'

III.

A S in the snowy stillness,
    Where the stars shine greenly
  In a mirror of ice,
The reindeer abideth alone,
And fleeth swiftly
From her following shadow
    In the moon,—
I speed for ever
From the shape abhorrèd
That my mind projects,
And my soul believes;
And I loom for ever
Through desolate regions
Of wondrous thought;
And I fear the thing
That follows me,
And cannot escape it
    Night or day.

Doth thy wingéd lightning
Strike, O Master!

The reindeer flying
        Her shade?
Will Thy wrath pursue me,
Because I cannot
Escape the shadow
Of the thing I am?

I have pried and pondered,
I have agonized,
I have sought to find Thee,
        Yet still must roam,
Affrighted, fleeing Thee,
Chased by the shadow
Of the thing I am,
Through desolate regions
Of wondrous thought'

IV.

BECAUSE Thou art beautiful,
　Because Thou art mysterious,
　Because Thou art strong,
Or because Thou art shadowy,
Shall my soul worship Thee,
　O thou Unseen One?

As men bow to monarchs,
As servants to masters,
　Shall I bow to Thee?
As one that is fearful,
As one that is insolent,
　Shall I pray to Thee?

Wert Thou a demigod,
Wert Thou an angel,
　Prayer-worship might serve;
To Thee, most beautiful,

31

Wondrous, mysterious,
   How shall it avail?

Thou art not a monarch,
Thou art not a master,—
   Why should I bow to Thee?
I am not fearful,
I am not insolent,—
   Why should I pray to Thee?

Enough, if Thou beest,
Gently and humanly
   To ask if Thou art?
To worship and wonder at,
Pray to and strive with,
   The wonders which be?

V.

SOUL AND BODY.

M Y Soul, thou art wed
To a perishable thing,
But death shall dissolve
Thee and thy slimy mate.
If thou wilt reap wings,
Take all thy mate can give.

The touch of the smelling dead
The kiss of the maiden's mouth,
The sorrow, the hope, the fear,
That floweth along her flesh:
Take all, nor be afraid;
Cling close to thy mortal mate!

So shalt thou duly wring
Out of thy foul embrace
The hunger and thirst whereof

The Master maketh thee wings,
The beautiful wondrous yearning,
The mighty thirst to endure.

Be not afraid, my soul,
To leave thy mate at last,
Though thou shalt learn in time
To love each other well;
But put her gently down
In the earth beneath thy feet.

And dry thine eyes, and hasten
To the imperishable springs;
And it shall be well for thee,
In the beautiful Master's sight,
If it be found in the end
Thou hast used her tenderlie.

VI.

M ASTER, if there be Hell,
    All men are bereaven!
If, in the universe,
One spirit receive the curse,
  How is there Heaven?
If there be hell for one,
Thou, Master, art undone.

Were I a soul in heaven,
  Afar from pain,
Yea, on Thy breast of snow,
At the scream of one below
  I should scream again.
Art Thou less piteous than
The conception of a man?

VII.

H E heard a voice, 'How should God pardon sin?
How should He save the sinner with the sinless?'
That would be ill: the LORD my GOD is just.

Further he heard, 'How shall GOD pardon lust?
How should he smile on the adulteress?'
That would be ill: the LORD my GOD is just.

Further he heard, 'How should GOD pardon blood?
How should the murtherer have a place in heaven
Beside the innocent life he took away?'

And GOD was on His throne; and in a dream
Saw small things making figures out of clay,
Shapen like men, and calling them GOD's justice.

And saw the shapes look up into His eyes,
Exclaiming, 'Thou dost ill to save this man;
Damn Thou this woman, and curse this cutthroat, LORD!'

GOD dreamt this, and His dreaming was the world;
And Thou and I are dreams within His dream;
And nothing dieth GOD hath dreamt or thought.

VIII.

'SAD, and sweet, and wise,
　　Here a babe reposes;
Dust is on his eyes,
Quietly he lies,—
　　Satan, strew roses!'

Weeping low, creeping slow,
　　Came the weary-wingéd;
Roses red over the dead
　　Quietly he flingéd.

'I am old,' he thought,
　　'And the world's day closes.
Pale and fever-wrought.
Darkly have I wrought
　　These blood-red roses.'

By his side the mother came,
　　Shudderingly creeping;

The Devil's and the woman's heart
   Bitterly were weeping.

'Sweet he came, and swift he flew;
   Hopeless he reposes:
Waiting on is weary too,—
Wherefore on his grave we strew
   Bitter withering roses.'

The Devil gripped the woman's heart,
   With gall he staunched its bleeding.
Far away beyond the day
   The LORD heard interceding.

'LORD GOD, One in Three!
   Sure Thy anger closes:
Yesterday I died, and see
The weary-wingéd over me
   Bitterly streweth roses!'

The voice cried out, 'Rejoice! rejoice!
   There shall be sleep for evil;'
And all the sweetness of GOD's voice
   Passed rustling through the Devil.

32

IX.

IN the time of my tribulation
Melt me, Master, like snow;
Melt me, dissolve me, exhale me,
Into thy wool-white cloud;
With a warm wind blow me upward
Over the hills and the seas,
And upon a summer morning
Poise me over the valley
Of Thy mellow yellow realm;
Then, for a wondrous moment,
Watch me from infinite space
With Thy round red eyeball of sunlight,
And melt and dissolve me downward
In the beautiful silver rain
That drippeth musically,
With a gleam like starlight and moonlight,
On the footstool of Thy throne.

DALZIELS' FINE ART BOOKS.

ROBERT BUCHANAN.

Superb binding, designed by Albert Warren, One Guinea; or, Morocco elegant and antique, Thirty-six Shillings.

WAYSIDE POSIES.

ORIGINAL POEMS OF THE COUNTRY LIFE.

EDITED BY ROBERT BUCHANAN,
Author of ' London Poems,' ' Idyls of Inverburn,' etc.

Pictures by G. J. PINWELL, J. W. NORTH, and FREDERICK WALKER,

Engraved by the Brothers Dalziel.

NOTICES OF THE PRESS.

'Of sketches, poetical as well as pictorial, there are, as might be expected, many in this book.'—*Athenæum.*

'Both poets and artists have used their opportunity well.'—*Saturday Review.*

'The book is well printed, well bound, and altogether looks very handsome.'—*Pall Mall Gazette.*

'So far as our observation of the "gift-books" of the season has hitherto extended, this, perhaps, takes precedence of all others in the beauty of its illustrations, upwards of forty in number.'—*Art Journal.*

'Of late years we have seen nothing in the way of landscape drawing to approach these woodcuts of Mr. North's; they will recommend themselves by their graceful novelty of subject and the vigour of a quite new "touch." The illustrations, for instance, to the poems called "Afloat on the Stream," "Reaping," and "The Heath," are marvels of truth and delicate workmanship. Mr. F. Walker and Mr. Pinwell are very happy in several of their subjects, and the cutting of all the drawings seems to have been done with great faithfulness and delicacy by Messrs. Dalziel. The volume altogether is a handsome and beautiful one—admirably printed and tastefully bound.'—*Morning Star.*

'The whole book is worthy of the highest commendation as respects the mechanical as well as its literary qualities. The handsome exterior covers about a hundred extremely thick leaves, which are printed on only one side in the most superior manner. By what we presume is a new process, the printed page has been tinted in the centre only, leaving a wide margin of pure white round the letterpress and prints. The volume is certainly the handsomest specimen of printer's and binder's work which we have seen. The illustrations number among them many of Mr. F. Walker's drawings, charming for their accuracy of representation. His picture on page 3 is a perfect study; indeed, all his figures have the very turn of nature about them. The contributions of Mr. J. W. North are only less excellent.'—*Sunday Gazette.*

'May both be commended and recommended '—*Daily Telegraph.*

'Certainly a most sumptuous volume, in which all concerned in its production have done their utmost.'—*Globe.*

'This is a really first-rate book in every respect, and, moreover, considering the labour and cost expended on it, a cheap book.'—*Standard.*

'Too much praise cannot be accorded to the manipulation of the various pictures by the Brothers Dalziel. They have executed their share of the work with all their accustomed delicacy of touch and appreciation of the original designs.'—*Morning Post.*

DALZIELS' FINE ART BOOKS.

ROBERT BUCHANAN.

In chaste binding, small 4to., gilt and gilt edges, Ten Shillings and Sixpence.

BALLAD STORIES

OF THE

AFFECTIONS.

FROM THE SCANDINAVIAN.

BY ROBERT BUCHANAN,

Author of ' London Poems,' ' Idylls of Inverburn,' etc.

With Illustrations by G. J. PINWELL, J. D. WATSON, J. LAWSON, T. DALZIEL, A. B. HOUGHTON, E. DALZIEL, W. SMALL, &c.

Engraved by the Brothers Dalziel.

NOTICES OF THE PRESS.

' We have thus referred to this excellent collection of fanciful images, strange turns of invention, and intensely dramatic pictures, in order to express our sense of the author's good fortune in putting so many treasures before the public: the latter will welcome his success with a new sense of pleasure and obligation to one who has so often done well in his own person.'—*Athenæum.*

' Every page is true poetry of the old ballad kind, and nearly all the modern ballads of Oehlenschläger are complete little works of rare art. "The Treasure-Seeker," especially, is a poetic gem that will delight all who read it.'—*Spectator.*

' We do not know a ballad more vigorous and intense than "Ebbe Skammelson." It reminds us of what Sir Philip Sidney said of " Chevy Chase,"—that it stirred him like a trumpet. The book is profusely illustrated, in what is now the popular style—a quaint and stern realism,—which suits these old-world stories. The book, as a whole, is a beautiful and dainty gift-book, and will doubtless secure a large amount of favour.'—*The British Quarterly Review.*

' Mr. Buchanan beautifies all that he touches upon in verse. Here are subjects which test the ring of the metal whereof he is made, and the sound comes out sharp and clear.' —*Standard.*

' We heartily welcome and commend these renderings of Scandinavian poetry, and only wish that Mr. Buchanan could be persuaded to go on with this sort of work.'—*Daily Telegraph.*

' "Axel and Walborg," the longest ballad in the volume, is also, perhaps, the finest ; but Oehlenschläger's " Children in the Moon," is exquisite, and is, moreover, exquisitely translated. Indeed, none but a true poet could possibly have wrought some of the translations in this interesting volume. The book is beautifully printed and richly illustrated.' —*Morning Star.*

DALZIELS' FINE ART BOOKS.

Ten Shillings and Sixpence.
Handsome binding, full gilt.

ODES AND SONNETS;

SELECTED FROM OUR BEST ENGLISH POETS.

Illustrated with Tinted Pictures by BIRKET FOSTER, and Ornamental
Designs by J. SLIEGH,

Engraved and Printed by the Brothers Dalziel.

'The book is a remarkable specimen, not only of the engraving, but of the printing of
the Brothers Dalziel.'—*Times.*

Seven Shillings and Sixpence.
Elaborate illuminated binding, small 4to., gilt edges.

GRISET'S GROTESQUES;

OR,

JOKES DRAWN ON WOOD, WITH RHYMES BY TOM HOOD.

One Hundred quaint Designs by ERNEST GRISET,

Engraved by the Brothers Dalziel.

'Griset is certainly a most humorous artist, and his free-hand sketches are as clever as
they are grotesque and laughable.'—*Art Journal.*

'"Griset's Grotesques" is wealthy in nonsensical fun.'—*Athenæum.*

NEW EDITION, Two Shillings and Sixpence ;
Bevelled boards and gilt edges, Three Shillings and Sixpence.

AN OLD FAIRY TALE:

THE SLEEPING BEAUTY.

BY RICHARD DOYLE AND J. R. PLANCHE.

'Of all the old fairy tales this is surely the most fascinating and the most suggestive, and
it is here told anew and versified by Mr. Planché, who has made the region of fairy extrava-
ganza his own peculiar domain. Mr. Doyle's drawings are delightful as ever.'—*Times.*

Three Shillings and Sixpence.
Extra cloth gilt and gilt edges, on fine toned paper.

PICTURE FABLES.

*One Hundred Engravings by the Brothers Dalziel, from Original Designs
by* OTTO SPECKTER.

WITH RHYMES FROM THE GERMAN OF F. HEY,
Translated by H. W. DULCKEN, Ph.D.

'It is difficult to say whether the designs of Otto Speckter or the Rhymes of Hey are the
most charming. The book is exquisitely got up, and a marvel of cheapness.'